ASHER

The Mavericks, Book 5

Dale Mayer

Books in This Series:

ASHER: THE MAVERICKS, BOOK 5
Dale Mayer
Valley Publishing Ltd.

Copyright © 2019

ISBN-13: 978-1-773362-11-3
Print Edition

About This Book

What happens when the very men—trained to make the hard decisions—come up against the rules and regulations that hold them back from doing what needs to be done? They either stay and work within the constraints given to them or they walk away. Only now, for a select few, they have another option:

The Mavericks. A covert black ops team that steps up and break all the rules ... but gets the job done.

Welcome to a new military romance series by USA Today best-selling author Dale Mayer. A series where you meet new friends and just might get to meet old ones too in this raw and compelling look at the men who keep us safe every day from the darkness where they operate—and live—in the shadows ... until someone special helps them step into the light.

A born protector, Asher signs up for jobs even the most trained men won't take ...

But finding a set of female autistic twins in mainland China—after someone has gone to a great deal of effort to make sure they are never found—isn't easy. Finding those responsible behind the actual kidnapping is even harder ...

Mickie, hired to look after the twins for the last six months, is still recovering from the trauma of being beaten and drugged, waking to find her adult charges gone. Beside herself already, then seeing Asher, her ex from ten years ago, is another sock to her gut. And to her heart. ... She's not the same person she was back then and, being with him again, shows her just how much she'd screwed up her relationship with him.

Yet betrayal, deceit and bodies litter their pathway as they struggle to save the missing women before the kidnapper's assassins get close enough to take them out instead ...

Sign up to be notified of all Dale's releases here!
https://smarturl.it/DaleNews

CHAPTER 1

A SHER TROMBLAY WALKED along Coronado Beach, wondering at the strange turn of his life. He was leaving Coronado, and this was his goodbye walk. Technically he was already no longer part of the naval world, and, after doing that job to help out Beau, Asher would head off on his own mission next. He just didn't know when and didn't know how. He'd already gotten rid of everything in his life except for a small sterile apartment in San Diego, and that was it. But then he didn't want anything more.

It was so strange to be at this stage. When he entered the military and became a Navy SEAL, he never thought about life after the navy. Most men only lasted eight, maybe ten years. Asher had crossed that line himself now. The guys on the Mavericks team had all found something else to do with themselves, and he had too. More of the same, just better.

Just then his phone rang. He looked down and read the Caller ID. *Mavericks*. He laughed at that. "Asher here."

"You ready?" Beau was on the other end.

Asher took a deep breath. "Ready? Where am I going?"

"How do you feel about Asia?"

He frowned at that. "After those girls sold into the sex trade?"

"Well, you're going after somebody else over there," Beau said. "We think it's connected to the same deal we just came off of in Alaska, but that's not the main concern. We are still working on that, but it's not the focus of your mission."

"Well, it should be a pretty big concern," Asher said.

"Maybe," he said. "What we've got is a set of twins."

"Great," he said with a laugh. "What age?"

"They're thirty. They were picked up at their hotel room in Shanghai and apparently are being held for ransom somewhere in China."

"What connections do they have to the Alaska cult?"

"None directly but maybe they intersect with another human trafficking ring or sex-trade black market operation. The twins are models," he said. "Their mother is a highly sought after wedding planner for the rich and famous and was in China to research and to prepare for a high-profile wedding in Shanghai."

"Why would the twins be kidnapped?" Asher asked.

"We're hearing all kinds of theories. Maybe it's a political statement. No clue. If you're ready to go, you leave in five hours."

"Well, I'm going," he said, "but my Chinese sucks."

"You'll have a partner on the other side this time."

"And who's that?" he asked.

"Ryker. And another person will be helping out."

"Who are we thinking has the twins?"

"I could be wrong, but the most direct link among the theories, consistent with the facts at hand, is that the mother has some client—either a current one or a hopeful future one—holding the twins captive, forcing the mother to take on the planning of some upcoming wedding."

"Well, that brings up a whole new meaning to *bridezilla*," Asher said, but no laughter was in his voice. He turned to face the ocean sprawled in front of him. "And these are thirty-year-old twins?"

"Yes. We understand they're autistic."

"Are they difficult to handle?"

"Yes. Probably so. At the same time, you must keep your eyes and ears open in case you hear any information on the sex traffickers."

"We never did get any of that rundown after the Alaska op, did we?"

"The Mavericks team is working on it. They got a line on one supply chain."

"Is this connected?"

"No, I don't think so. Not from what we've got so far. But it would be nice to have closure."

"And you, are you heading out on another job?"

"No. I'm here as your central communication center."

"Are we ever doing team missions?"

"We help one person do a job, and then we're into team jobs."

"If you say so," Asher said. "Did you ever think about quitting?"

"Before? All the time," he said. "But it's different now. We get to say no sometimes. We get to say yes sometimes. The budget is there. The decisions are ours—not the brass above us."

"I get it," Asher said. "Makes a whole lot of sense in many ways."

"So, are you up for this?"

"I'm up for it," he said. "How am I getting there?"

"Military transport, various kinds, disembarking at a US military base in South Korea."

"And from there?"

"And from there," he said, "you're on your own."

"My backup will be there?"

"Your backup plus one will be there," Beau said.

"Who's the plus-one?"

"Her name is Mickie," he said.

"I only know one woman named Mickie," Asher said. "It better not be her."

"Yep. Sorry. It's her. She's the private nurse for the twins."

And then Beau was gone, leaving Asher staring at the phone in shock. Mickie was his ex-fiancée from his early days in the military. While she'd finished nursing school, he'd gone into SEALs training, and then, she'd gone into Doctors without Borders.

What the hell was she doing in Asia on this assignment as a family nurse and as his plus-one? That didn't bear thinking about.

Of all the women in the world he wanted to see again, she was not one.

CHAPTER 2

A SHER HAD HITCHED an undocumented ride on a US military cargo plane across the Pacific Ocean, arriving in the wee hours this morning, now Tuesday, having jumped over the rest of his Monday into his new time zone here, to slip his way on board a nearby navy ship to crash for a few hours. He now stood on the deck of the USS *Chosin* and stared at the town in front of him as the sun rose. He was docked at the US base in South Korea. Nobody was allowed to know he was here. Nobody was allowed to know he was leaving. Such was his current life. But then, as he had no end of files on his cell phone and a disk in his fingers and a laptop in his backpack, that was about all the help he would get.

Except for his backup plus one. That still really bothered him that Mickie was his plus-one. He couldn't imagine what was going on there, but the order had been given. It was up to him whether to follow that order, but this was the only order he had. And maybe he could live with that. The trouble was, this op was a lot of responsibility on his shoulders. Thankfully he had a backup. *Ryker.* Asher just didn't know where his partner was yet. He took several deep breaths of the fresh morning air and then walked down the disembark plank.

Once on the boardwalk, he kept walking. Several others

had disembarked with him. Asher was a little more obvious in that he wasn't in uniform. He had deliberately kept to the center of the crowd. He had gear with him that he would need to set up, but he wanted to be on land and away from the base first. Something about working mostly alone had him looking at everybody, including other servicemen, even navy seamen, as potentially being part of the problem. If Asher was the solution, who else was out there? And what were they doing? And were they on his side or somebody else's side?

He shrugged and moved forward.

As soon as his group reached an open area, he could see more and more crowds filing in to meet up with the seamen just getting off. Asher stepped to the side, slipped around the corner of a building, and headed toward Seoul, but his real destination was the Port of Incheon area. He wanted to reach Shanghai as soon as he could. He'd done some research on the best method of travel to get him into China, and flying seemed the fastest and the easiest.

Except he wanted nobody to see his face, so a private boat would be the better option to sneak him in. His backpack was full of cash, and he could access more if he needed it. He headed along the edge of the walkway, his gaze covertly searching the whole area. He would recognize his backup.

As soon as he separated a little more from the group, his gaze caught sight of a tall male, dressed all in black, leaning against the ropes up ahead, his face turned away from Asher. That set of shoulders. That haircut. Even though it had grown out, it was still short. Asher walked up and passed him and said, "Good morning." This man was yet another old friend of his. Inside, he was grinning.

Ryker stepped in behind him. As soon as they were in among the buildings, Ryker, beside Asher now, said, "We have a boat."

"Good," Asher said. "Do we need other supplies first?"

"No, we have pretty much everything we need from here, and, what we don't have, we can pick up in China."

"Good enough." China was well-known for having anything and everything available for a price. And it wasn't even all that expensive. Within minutes, they turned onto a smaller dock where a good half-dozen boats were tied up. One of them looked more like a speedboat than anything. He assumed that was his. But, no, Ryker took Asher to another, a fishing boat.

Ryker hopped in. "Grab the line, will you?"

Asher quickly untied the knot from the dock and tossed the rope into the back of their boat; then he stepped in as well and moved forward. Ryker turned on the engine and put out toward the open sea. As Asher looked around, this boat was just one of many and was a whole lot more inconspicuous than the speedboat would have been, although the speedboat would have been faster.

As soon as they were out and away from everybody, Ryker turned, looked at him, and said, "You might want to sit down."

Asher raised his eyebrows but sat down in the passenger seat as Ryker opened up the throttle, and the engine surged forward. Asher let out a laugh because, under cover of a fishing boat camouflage was one very sweet engine.

Ryker shouted over the wind, "Totally different deal this time, isn't it?"

"Yes," he said, "but I'm liking it."

"Did you ever do much undercover work?"

Asher shrugged. "Not enough. This is definitely what I prefer."

"Me too," Ryker said. After that, they just shared silence for a long time.

Finally Asher had to ask, "I heard we have a plus-one?"

Ryker nodded. "But Mickie is not here. She's in Shanghai."

"Okay," he said slowly, still stunned she was involved at all. "So why were the twins in Shanghai when they were taken, yet the mother was working on some China wedding?"

Ryker laughed. "I think the first stopover was China. Then the second part of the trip had them in Shanghai."

"Okay," Asher said, still considering this new information. "Do we know why Mickie is with us?"

"She was separated from the twins," Ryker said. "When they were kidnapped, she was knocked out and drugged heavily. When she came to, the police didn't appear to care too much about what had happened. Then the mother contacted somebody who contacted the Mavericks and set her up with us."

"And the advantage of having Mickie is what?"

"Apparently, when we grab the twins, they can be a little difficult," Ryker said.

"As anybody with special needs can be. Hell, I can be on any given day," Asher said with a nod. "So maybe it did make sense that she was there. But I'm surprised. She's doing private nursing?"

"I don't know anything about it," Ryker said. "She was a nurse with Doctors without Borders in the past. I know that much, but apparently now she's doing this."

Asher wasn't even sure what *this* was, but it had been a

good eight years since he'd seen her and ten years since they were engaged.

Ryker glanced at him. "Problems?"

Asher's smile slid sideways. "No, we have a history. That's all."

Ryker chuckled. "Of course you do. It's not like anything would ever be easy."

"It was a long time ago. We were very young."

"Got it," Ryker said. "Chances are she's married with half-a-dozen kids already."

That threw Asher. If she was, she surely wouldn't be hired as a live-in private nurse outside of the States, would she? But no point in asking questions nobody could answer. Much better to wait and see how the chips fell. He was a professional. His job was to return the twins safely to their family. According to his notes, home was in Geneva.

And then he thought about Mickie and Geneva and realized that her gig made more sense than he thought. Because Mickie's grandmother had been Swiss, and the last time he'd seen her grandmother, she was in good health but aging rapidly. Maybe Mickie had left the Doctors without Borders organization to look after her grandmother? Again he found himself questioning and doubting the circumstances when there was really no point. They'd get answers soon enough. Hopefully first thing this afternoon when they reached Shanghai.

MICHAELLA HUNKER, MICKIE for short, waited impatiently in a small hotel in Shanghai. She couldn't sleep, and she kept checking the time. Currently it was just before one p.m.,

Tuesday, the day after the kidnapping. Actually about thirty-six hours later. But she had been drugged for the first eight hours, which was a blessing of sorts, cutting short her actual worry time, but she hated that the twins were in the hands of their kidnappers for so long. For too long.

This was definitely not Mickie's first choice of location for a meet, given the kidnapping of the twins from here, but the twins' mother, Chandra, had ordered Mickie to await the US team coming to help, while Chandra had promptly booked herself into another hotel. So Mickie had been trapped here another twenty-eight hours, given the team's flight time of around twelve hours and another eight for a secret boat ride into Shanghai, not to mention the five-hour delay before the team's plane even left the States and maybe a short nap had been thrown in there somewhere too. She just hoped, with the time zone changes involved—some fifteen to sixteen hours ahead of California's time zone—that this team was well rested and had no jet lag issues.

She'd been on the oceans around here several times during her stints with Doctors without Borders. But after Mickie left that organization to look after her grandmother, her life had been at a much more sedate pace. And yet, she still found herself automatically reverting to some of her automatic responses during her years with Doctors without Borders. As in hating the crowds here, yet loving the atmosphere.

But, at the same time, that seemed like a lifetime away. Her grandmother had passed away six months ago after a two-and-a-half-year-long illness, where Mickie had been at her side every day. That loss hurt so badly that Mickie hadn't wanted to stick around the empty house. Said empty house had been left to her, along with enough money that she didn't have to work, but she didn't want to sit there with the memories and the pain and the grief rolling through her.

So, when one of her grandmother's friends had asked Mickie to help look after the daughters—Amelia and Alisha—of a famous wedding planner she knew, Mickie had agreed. The twins were autistic but, due to their ethereal beauty, had done a stint at modeling and had taken the world by storm.

Mickie's predecessor, Lana, had been with the girls for over a decade—managing their day-to-day schedule and care—until she and Chandra had had a falling out. Chandra's son, Edward, had urged his mother to fire Lana. So Mickie took over and was currently completing a trial six-month contract with the family. That contract was just about up, and, of course, everything blew up at the end.

She and the twins and their mother had been booked into a famous and well-respected hotel in Shanghai—the same one Mickie was required to stay in now—when a knock came at the door. Not suspecting anything wrong, Mickie had walked over and opened the door to find two gunmen. She'd been knocked out almost immediately. Later the morning of the kidnapping, about eight a.m. on Monday, the hotel's housekeeping staff had found her, still knocked out and tied up on the floor beside the bed, yet the twins were gone. One of the twins was a diabetic, and the other one dealt with never-ending stomach issues.

The twins had been kidnapped, and Mickie had been dumped. She wished she'd been taken with them. At least then she could have maintained their health, helped to keep them calm, if not safe. She worried about what could happen to them. Why were the twins taken? Blackmail? Ransom? Their mother was well-known and wealthy. So trying to grab a chunk of her money made sense.

Since the twins and Chandra were Americans by birth and the local authorities were of no help, she had called in for a US team. Mickie just didn't know who was being sent or how many would be in their team.

After several more rounds of pacing, she collapsed on the bed. Chandra had told Mickie not to leave the hotel room, the scene of the crime—in case the twins found their way back here, plus to meet the team Chandra had hired—and the walls were crowding in on Mickie. A knock sounded on the door. She straightened up slowly, and the knock came again.

When a voice she recognized from the dim recesses of her mind called out to her, she raced to the door and opened it. She stared at Asher in shock. He put one finger to his lips and then slipped inside with another man beside him. The door was shut and locked; then he went to the windows, and immediately the second man pulled out a device and checked her room over.

She realized just how much more serious this could get. When the second man finally said, "All clear," Asher turned, looked at her, and said, "Good afternoon, Mickie."

She shook her head. "You?"

He shrugged. "Why not me?"

She didn't have an answer. She didn't have any answers.

"Before we get into this heartwarming reunion," the other man said, "I'm Ryker. Nice to meet you. What can you tell us about what happened?"

And, just like that, it became all-business right from the start. She sagged onto the bed again and explained it once more.

"Do the kidnappers know about the medical conditions

of the twins?" Ryker asked.

She shrugged. "I don't know."

"This is about a wedding?" Asher asked in confusion.

"I don't know that either. It seems far-fetched to me, but I know that weddings at this level cost upward of one million dollars." Asher just stared at her, and she could see the shock registering in his eyes. She nodded. "And I think that's why, when Chandra refused a potential client because her schedule is booked for five years …"

His jaw dropped a little more. "Seriously?"

She nodded. "You must remember. We're talking about the megarich here."

"Right," he said, swallowing with great difficulty. "And maybe something else is behind it that we don't know about."

"It's hard to say," she noted. "I highly doubt the future bride will have any inclination to speak up if there's any truth to it."

"We do find, when people explain their actions, which we later find out are lies, that they are involved for a very unrelated reason," Ryker said.

"And I was thinking about that too," she said. "We were at their home in Switzerland for the longest time, and then Chandra came to do research on two upcoming weddings—one in Japan in four months for the prime minister's niece and another in China in eight months that she had promised to do for the president's granddaughter. We landed first in Japan, then came to China."

Asher, his arms crossed, asked, "And the twins traveled with their mother all the time?"

Mickie shook her head. "In the six months I've worked for her, I haven't done any traveling. And Chandra had been gone most of the time. I don't know why she brought the twins this time."

"Were they happy to come?"

She shook her head. "No, they weren't. They don't like traveling. They want everything the same. They thrive on routine. They hate change and are getting worse in that regard. They like the things that they know, the places that they recognize, the food that they love. They are truly happy when home, in Geneva, in their garden, with their pets. They are miserable when you take them out of that environment. And it brings on more tantrums and emotional outbursts."

"So then we need to find out from Chandra why she brought them to Japan and China."

"And I've asked," Mickie said, "but she hasn't given me a decent answer."

"That's where we start then," Asher said. "Do you know where she is?" As he spoke, he glanced at his watch. She remembered that about him from before; he was very time conscious.

"No," she said. "She left me her cell phone though."

"Her cell phone?"

"Yes, she's in incredibly high demand. Her office handles most of the calls. Anybody who's dealing with her on a personal level has a phone number to call her directly."

"Interesting." He held out his hand.

She gave him the phone and asked, "Does she know you're here?"

"To the best of my knowledge," Asher said, "she's the one who brought us in."

CHAPTER 3

MICKIE STARED AT the man she'd loved, since forever, trying to see the younger man inside this older, seasoned warrior. But it was hard. She found no twinkle of laughter in his gaze. More lines were around the corner of his mouth. His forehead and jaw were more sculpted, but the tick was still there. The tick in the corner of his jaw as he studied the phone in his hand. She used to reach up and kiss it all the time, telling him that he needed to calm down before that became a permanent feature of his face.

Apparently he hadn't calmed down because it was there right now. He'd filled out a lot more than she remembered too. His forearms and biceps were massive. He wore a T-shirt, but it looked like it was two sizes too small. Then again he'd always had trouble fitting in clothes. If they fit in one spot, they didn't fit in another. He stared at the phone, hit a button, and held it to his ear. When a woman answered on the other end, he said, "We're in China. Where are you?" He looked over at Ryker and nodded. "We'll come to you."

He turned and walked toward the door. Mickie bolted to her feet, slipped on sandals, and said, "I'm coming with you."

He looked at Ryker, who returned his stare and then shrugged.

"It wouldn't be my choice to have you with us," Asher

said.

Immediately she felt hurt wobble inside. She hadn't expected it to be him in the first place. She'd seen him maybe eight years ago, totally by accident, at an event. But that had been all since they broke up their relationship a decade ago.

"It doesn't matter what you think on this subject," she said. "If there's any chance of finding the twins between here and there or at any location, I need to come."

"Are you bringing your black medical bag too?"

Her first thought was it might have been an insult, but his expression held interest and curiosity, not mockery. She reached down, grabbed her large purse, and threw it over her shoulder. "It's all in here."

"Good," he said. "Then come." But then he stopped, looking at her and pointed at her small travelling bag.

"The rest of my things will be fine," she said with a frown. "I don't really have much else with me."

At that, his lips turned down, as if critiquing her very casual clothing. "We'll take it anyway."

"I'm not a warrior like you," she muttered. "I'm a nurse."

He nodded, picked up her bag and opened the door, letting her step out in front of him. The hotel door was locked, but Asher had spent a little longer at the door than necessary. She frowned at him, but he ignored her. That was something else she wasn't used to. Normally he was very attentive. Always there for her. She had to remember why it was that they'd broken up because all she remembered right now were the good times.

The men said something behind her, but she didn't hear what it was. When she turned, they had already moved rapidly past her and toward the elevator.

"Are you coming?" Asher asked.

They'd walked right by her, and she still stood in the hallway staring at Asher. She gave her head a shake and said, "Yes," and ran after them.

Once outside, the whole time they walked along the street to Chandra's hotel, Asher was busy checking blueprints on his cell. Ryker had gone ahead, only she didn't know where.

Mickie walked at Asher's side. "What are you doing?" she asked curiously.

"Checking for exits. Checking for cameras. Making sure we're not walking into a trap."

"Can you really do that from out here? So far away?"

"I can make a best-guess effort," he said. "But, if it's a well-laid trap, it's pretty hard for anybody to fail-safe that."

"That doesn't make me feel any better."

"It's not meant to," he said. "You were targeted. Or rather the three of you were. They dealt with you very efficiently and took what they wanted."

As if that didn't make her feel even guiltier. "Must you say it like that?" she asked, hating that her voice trembled.

He looked up, surprised. "Like what?"

"Like you blame me too," she said. "Isn't it bad enough that I'm racked with guilt already?"

"Didn't you say that they came in through the hotel room door with guns, and they were obviously well-trained?"

She nodded.

"You're what? Five-five, 130 pounds?"

Again she nodded, hating the fact that he'd hit the number right on the head. She'd been trying to lose a little bit of weight, but it hadn't seemed all that important. Until now, ... damn it.

"You couldn't have done anything then," he said gently. "Short of having killer martial arts skills and hidden weapons, what would you do?"

"Of which I don't have either," she said, "so I did nothing because I couldn't."

"Just acknowledge what happened and move on," he said. "They won't get a second chance."

"You'll protect me?" she asked drily. "I'd have thought you'd throw me to the wolves."

He jumped, turned to look at her, and asked, "Why would I do that?"

And left her feeling foolish.

⚓

ASHER WASN'T SURE what was going on in Mickie's head, but he didn't have time for it. He'd compartmentalized his brain and had safely put Mickie back where she belonged. In his past. They had had a great thing, and they had chosen to break it off. They'd each gone their own way. The end. At least it would be if she stayed where she'd been put. Only that wasn't Mickie's style.

At Chandra's hotel, Asher immediately headed straight for the front reception desk. He could sense Mickie's surprise at the directness of his approach. He nodded at the front desk clerk and said, "We're heading up to see Chandra Chancer." The name had helped her establish her CC brand.

The man picked up the phone in an instant and said in stiff English, "I must report your presence."

"That's good," he said with a big smile. "Make sure you tell everybody."

At that, the man looked at him and said, "Sorry?"

But Asher waved a hand. "Not to worry." Then he turned and snagged Mickie's arm and tucked it into his and headed toward the elevator.

"What was that all about?" she whispered as soon as they were inside. She watched as the door opened at another floor, but he quickly shut it, stopping anybody else from getting on with them. "Wow. You really don't like to share, do you?"

"No," he said. "You should remember that well. Not that I was possessive. More that I wanted as much time with you as I could." *Shit. She wouldn't stay put.* "I'm sorry. Obviously I don't have this all packaged up in my history as well as I thought it was."

"No," she snapped. "That was a low blow."

He acknowledged it with a quick nod and said, "Sorry. It won't happen again."

Inside, he was like, *Damn it. You definitely will do that again.*

"And, just for the record," she said, "I never cheated. Nor do I like sharing."

"I know," he said. "I never cheated either."

"And trust wasn't the problem. I always trusted you," she said.

"Trust we had on both sides," he said. "That part we had down pat."

She winced at that.

He nodded. "It was a long time ago."

"I know," she said.

Just then the elevator opened, and he stepped out. He held an arm in front of her, stopping her from walking past. When he realized it was clear, he walked forward to the proper door and knocked. Instead of it being opened right away, the door behind them opened. He studied the gunman standing there, staring at him, and nodded. "Nice to see you again," Asher said. The man frowned. "You were at the elevators before us," he said.

Surprise lit the gunman's face. He crossed his arms over his chest.

Asher looked at him and said, "Are we allowed in or not?" But he said it in such a bored tone that she didn't quite understand what was going on. The gunman stepped to one side, and Asher walked into the big suite.

Immediately Mickie raced over to the older woman sitting on the settee, looking like she'd taken a massive blow to her life. Then again, she had. When your children were kidnapped and were particularly vulnerable ones, like these twins, life became that much more difficult.

Chandra looked up at Asher, gave him a half-broken smile, and said, "Thank you for coming."

He nodded and said, "First, I need to know why you brought them to Japan and China."

"It was a half-ditched effort to help educate them," she said. "I don't like coming to Asia, and I was looking at reducing my business, and I thought it would be one chance for them to see Tokyo and Shanghai. They are phenomenal cities, but the twins have become much more afraid lately."

"Afraid, why?" Asher asked. He could feel Mickie trying to reach out, mentally telling him to go easy, but he didn't have time for easy.

"I don't know," she said. "It's one of the reasons why I was cutting back my schedule. I hired Mickie here to stay with them all the time, so they wouldn't feel quite so isolated. But, being as they are, they often feel isolated anyway. As long as they have each other, they're okay. But lately it seemed like they were withdrawing more and more."

"So, you thought a trip halfway around the world, where you would be working all the time, would help?"

She gave a broken laugh. "Right. When you say it like that, it sounds nuts. If I wanted to get them out a little more, I should've taken them to Geneva for a day or over to England or up to Norway. Tokyo was such a shock to them that they refused to go anywhere but to stay in their hotel. The only thing they saw of the city was what could be seen from their hotel room window for the whole four days." He glanced at Mickie to confirm that.

Mickie nodded. "They were very unhappy with all of it. We traveled by private jet, but they didn't like that either."

Asher glanced back at the mother. "And why a private jet?"

She looked at him in surprise. "It's the only way I travel."

He nodded, thinking of the megarich again. "And I'll need information on anyone you've refused to plan a wedding for."

"Well, that's a lot more people now than before. My schedule is fully booked. I'm currently planning the wedding for the niece of the Japanese prime minister."

"So why are you in Shanghai?"

"I was trying to combine business trips. I have a wedding here in eight months. I wanted to get part of the details worked out. It's behind schedule already," she added crossly.

"Is it normal to plan two places at once?"

"Of course," she said. "Sometimes it's hard to find time for these long trips. As it is, I combine my travel as much as I can. At the end of this trip, I was supposed to be right here in Shanghai—to work, to plan, to research the next wedding on my plate. At the moment though, all my plans are on hold. I've told everybody I'm sick and not traveling right now."

"When is the wedding for the Japanese prime minister's niece?"

"Four months, so time is running out."

He stared at her for a long moment.

She looked up at him, her lips kinked up in the corner. "I get that you don't have anything to do with weddings, and I imagine you don't have anything to do with weddings at this level, but it does take one year to organize them, and I would much rather have two years."

His eyebrows rose at that.

She nodded. "Just accept it. This is a long-term industry. It's one of the reasons why I can't exactly cut down very quickly. I can say that I won't do any more weddings in the next five years, but I still must complete all my wedding commitments already made for the next five years regardless."

"So, if a person wanted you to do their wedding, how far in advance would they have to book it?"

She sighed. "Close to five years by now."

"That's a long wait for any engaged couple," he said.

"Exactly. So unfortunately some people book me in advance, when their son or daughter or whoever doesn't even have a partner yet."

He snorted, stared at her in shock.

She laughed. "I'm very exclusive, and I don't know who the nuptials are for until we get to the planning stage. And that's usually about a year and a half or two years out."

"Wow," he said, almost too stunned for words.

"They give me a nonrefundable deposit," she said. "And

that's half a million."

He kept from stumbling in response to all this rapid-fire information of a world he didn't understand. "So, say this person potentially didn't want to wait as long as you were saying. What would have happened if they had taken out one of your clients somewhere along the line?"

"If there's a cancellation," she said, "all funds, less expenses incurred up to that point in time, must be refunded, and then I jump to the next person in line."

"But surely dates have been set?"

"Yes, so the next couple is given a choice. If they wish to, they can move their wedding date ahead, or they can become a little more elaborate with their current wedding plans, as my time frees up."

"Do you ever squeeze anybody in?"

She winced at that. "I try not to do that, but it has happened, yes."

"So this kidnapping was somebody wanting to make sure that their wedding was next, is that it?"

"Maybe," she said.

"And what's this about the twins being models?"

"No," she said. "They *were* models for several years. They are beautiful with something special to their features, and they photograph wonderfully. But they're too high-strung and found it too difficult to deal with the lifestyle."

"Not to mention full-time careers?"

"They're fairly self-sufficient, or have been, within reason of course. They don't cook or anything like that," she said. "But the older they get, they want much less to do with that world."

"So they have money of their own?" He presumed they had maids or assistants for everything.

She nodded. "From their modeling, yes. I made sure it was invested so that they're taken care of, and, of course, I have money too."

"Do you have other children?"

"I have a son," she said. "He's a businessman in Geneva."

"Does he have anything to do with the twins?"

She hesitated, and he pounced. "The answer is no, I presume?"

She shrugged and said, "They don't get along."

"Is he younger or older?"

"He's younger but, of course, in many ways seems much older."

"So I'll ask a difficult question," he said. "Is there any chance that your son had anything to do with the kidnapping of the twins?"

She stared at him in shock, and then a visible tremor racked her body. She shook her head. "No, of course not." She frowned and looked at him in confusion. "And what's that got to do with the wedding I refused to plan?"

"I don't know for sure what *any* of this has to do with any wedding," he said calmly. "We often find that, in cases like this, it's all about what somebody wants."

"Yes," she said. "The future bride wants me to do her wedding."

"But you said it takes years to do it properly."

"Yes," she said; then she groaned. "Well, you might as well know all about it then."

"If you want our help," he said in barely restrained exasperation, "I need to know every detail."

"This woman came to me years ago. She was engaged. We set it up. She paid the deposit, and then she and her fiancé broke up. She canceled her spot, and I moved on."

"But now she's engaged again, and she wants her spot back?"

"Yes, and she wants the same wedding she had before. So, in many instances, everything is already designed, but we must rush the orders."

"What are the things that take the longest to order?"

"Well, honestly, if I have enough people and enough money, I could probably pull off a wedding in two weeks," she said. "Except for things that are pertinent to the bride, like her wedding dress. But, in this case, she already has it."

"And the wedding rings and all the other stuff?"

She nodded.

"So, because you said no, you wouldn't fit her in somewhere along the line …"

"She thought she'd go to the top of my list, which would be anytime now. We had a very difficult confrontation several months ago, and then I never heard from her again."

"And so you suspect she is behind the kidnapping of the twins."

"Well, she must be. Her name was on the ransom note."

His people had already dredged up her name and addresses, with a most likely one here in Shanghai. "And what's the ransom note say, exactly?" He had already seen a copy of it, but he wanted her take on it.

"She wants five million US dollars in cash within one week—which is now five days away—and the wedding to go off without a hitch and the world to not know what happened. Otherwise, she'll keep the twins. *They make great pets*," she added in disgust.

Asher still didn't understand the weeklong delay in the kidnapper getting their money. Something else was going on here. He'd run it by Ryker later. "And does any of that ring true for her?"

She shot him a hard look. "More than you know. She has an exotic pet collection."

"Ah. So that was a little personal touch, so you know that she meant business and that it was from her."

"Exactly."

"And, when we get the twins back, what will you do?"

"I'll make the ransom note public, and I'll make sure that she's no longer the fashion model she thinks she is and that her businesses go under."

"So she's not royalty. Does she have any big money or big families behind her who would hire another thirty odd gunmen to take you out?"

"No, ... not yet. But should you not find the twins in time, then she will have my five million dollars in five days. I've already gathered the cash, have it at one of the local banks, just awaiting her delivery instructions to come later," she said. "That's why I must destroy her. Otherwise, she would come back after me."

"Or you get the twins back and carry on with your day as if nothing happened," Mickie said from a chair beside them.

Asher looked at Mickie in surprise and then back at the mother.

"But she won't quit. You know that," Chandra said.

"Maybe a private message would be better than a public humiliation," Mickie said. "Or you could go to the police."

She laughed at that. "Everything is for sale here, particularly the police." Chandra sagged against the couch. "I need you to get them back, and I need them back fast."

"Were their medical conditions well-known?"

"Anybody from the modeling industry would have known. We always had somebody with them to make sure they took their medications."

"So then the kidnappers likely have a doctor with the twins to keep them in good health?"

"And I would presume that they're being handled with great care," Chandra said, "because my wrath, should anything happen to my daughters, would be horrific."

"And they'll know that?"

Chandra gave him a flat-out stare. "Young man, my skills are legendary. But my wrath beats out even that."

CHAPTER 4

M ICKIE NODDED. "THAT'S quite true. It's one of the reasons that she has fewer arguments than a lot of people who handle this level of weddings. Nobody wants to go up against her."

Chandra laughed bitterly. "And yet, years of cultivating that attitude seem to have backfired."

Mickie spotted Asher, already heading to the door. "Wait. Where are you going?"

He turned and looked at her in surprise. "To get the twins."

"Why? Don't you need anything else?"

He shrugged. "This is really best done with minimal force."

"You'll need me to look after them," she said, racing to his side.

"Maybe," he said. "If, in fact, they know you."

"They do." She glared at him. "I'm coming."

"The twins love her," Chandra said. "She's very good at calming them down."

He nodded. "Fine. But if she can't keep up ..." And he headed for the door.

Chandra anxiously called out, "Mickie, are you sure?"

Mickie waved back and said, "I'm fine. I've known Asher for a long time."

"If you say so," Chandra said. "I'd be happy to find more men to send along."

"Don't bother," Asher said, his voice hard. "They'll just get in my way."

Mickie followed him to the elevator. "I don't remember you being such a hard-ass."

"Circumstances," he said.

"Circumstances or me?"

He shrugged. "Not necessarily you. Although it was a bit of a surprise to find out you were here."

"Yeah. Apparently I'm the plus-one. Just in a work environment, not a personal one."

"Well, we tried that once. It didn't work so well. So here we can try the first one."

"It worked fine," she said.

He snorted. "So why'd we break up again?"

They went down the elevator, again with him refusing to let anybody else on. She watched his ability to keep that elevator door closed and shook her head. "You've done this a time or two."

"All the time."

When the door opened, she froze, staring at the loading dock area. "This isn't where I expected to get off."

"Yet it's where I expected to get off," he said calmly.

She groaned. "Yes, we did break up, but we were after different things."

"If you say so."

The breakup had been mostly her doing. "It was the right thing to do at the time," she said.

He stayed quiet, and she looked around and asked, "What happened to Ryker?"

Just then a small vehicle drove up beside them. Asher

30

reached for the back door of the vehicle, opened it, and said, "Get in. Ryker is driving." Surprised, she scrambled into the back seat before they took off and left her standing there.

As soon as he got in the front, Ryker asked Asher, "Did you learn anything?"

"Yes," Asher said. "I'm never getting married. Those weddings are nuts."

Ryker laughed. "You will when the time is right."

"I doubt it," Asher said. "Came close once. That was close enough."

That was a barb at her. Damn.

She sagged in her seat, wondering how she would get past this. Obviously Asher still had some hard feelings. Here and now wasn't exactly the time to talk to him about it. Back then she had thought it was the right thing to do, that she was holding him back, just like she felt now. Last time she'd opened the cage, and he'd taken his freedom. But, what if maybe, just maybe, what she had seen as him taking his freedom had actually been him feeling rejected and running? What the hell did she do with that? Of all the mistakes in her life, cutting ties between them was what she regretted most.

"Do we have a plan?" she asked, leaning forward between the two front seats.

"We need a secure hotel room, and we need blueprints and some weapons," Ryker responded instantly.

"Blueprints of?"

"Where this princess-type future bride is," Asher said. "We need to do reconnaissance first because I highly doubt the twins will be where the bride-to-be is currently living. More likely they've been stashed somewhere else."

"We need to get the video camera feeds from the hotel," Mickie suggested.

"Beau already got them," Ryker said. "They were disabled."

"Who's Beau?" she asked.

"Our contact person," Asher explained.

"The street cameras?" she asked.

"He's working on it. I need to check in." Asher opened up his laptop, did something funny to it as she watched from the back seat, and opened up a chat window.

She asked, "What about facial recognition?"

"We're on it," Asher said. "The trouble with the twins being models, their faces are still on various internet locations that they may not even be aware of." He quickly asked Beau for an update in the chat window. "So the kidnappers must keep the twins out of the public eye or risk them being recognized."

Going through city cameras right now, Beau typed. **We suspect that the twins were taken outside with hoods over their heads because of their notoriety.**

Suspect they were unconscious as well. In a vehicle with smoked windows.

Beau sent him a link.

Asher quickly clicked on it and up came a video camera feed. "Okay," he said. "We've got a video from the hotel garage." He watched as ten different vehicles left within about a ten-minute span. "Shit. Your hotel is really busy."

"They're checking all the vehicles that came and went at the time of the kidnapping?" she asked.

"Yes. This is a ten-minute piece that Beau's given us from around midnight." He looked back at Mickie. "Do you know when you were attacked?"

"It was probably about eleven that night," she said. "We had been late getting in."

"So you had just arrived here in Shanghai that day?"

"Yes," she said. "Our flights were all messed up. The

twins were very upset, and it was an extremely taxing day. By the time I got them up to the room, they were beyond done. So was I, for that matter."

INTO THE VIDEO camera feed again, Asher quickly checked and said, "Okay. We have you arriving at ten minutes past eleven and up to the room by twenty-five minutes past. The cameras went out at fifty minutes past. So, twenty-five minutes later, at twelve-fifteen, the camera system goes down, and, at twelve twenty-eight, the kidnappers have moved the twins into the vehicles underground." He scrolled through at superspeed, looking for anything potentially connected with the kidnapping.

Because two grown women were being moved, the trunk of a car wouldn't be enough, but that didn't eliminate one woman in the trunk and one on the back seat. He hit Stop when he came to a delivery van. He studied the interior and saw two men inside. Asher tried to zoom in for a closer image. *Interesting.* He took a screenshot and sent it to Beau. **See if we can identify these guys.** He had no way to turn the cameras to get a copy of the license plate, so Asher sent the full image and added, **Track this through the city.**

His chat window disappeared as Beau headed off to get the information they needed. "What do you think?" Asher asked Ryker. "A delivery van left just after midnight," he said. "Two men driving and dressed in black."

"Possible," Ryker said. "Doesn't mean it's them though."

"I'm still scanning," he muttered.

Just then they pulled up to Mickie's hotel.

CHAPTER 5

"DID WE TAKE a detour or a long way around?" Mickie asked.

"Yes," Ryker said. "To make sure we weren't followed."

"Got it," Asher said. "Beau tracked the van. More intel coming soon."

"While you're being so helpful," Mickie said, "any chance of food?"

"I'll order something up," Asher said, opening his passenger's side door.

She quickly jumped out of the car and followed him.

Still holding the laptop in his hands, Asher walked casually toward the elevators from the underground parking lot. The area was empty, dark. Their footsteps rang hollowly. But only two sets. Ryker had disappeared again.

She looked to see where he had gone, but she saw no sign of him. "Is he not coming with us?"

"He'll be back," Asher said quietly.

Then she realized that, although he held the laptop as if he were completely engrossed in whatever was on the screen, his gaze was checking out the entire area. She could feel shivers rocking down her spine as she noted just how intense his focus was. She really was out of her element. Resolutely determined to stay as far away from being a problem as she could, she stuck to his side.

"You'll still be in the way," he muttered, as if reading her thoughts.

"Maybe," she said, "but I'll do my best not to be."

In the elevator, he once again did something so they went straight up to the room, without the elevator stopping on any floor.

"Where are we going?"

"To my room," he said. It was on the tenth floor, and, as soon as the elevator doors were open, he checked the hallway. It was empty; then he typed something on the keyboard, and she watched his screen to see them appear. He opened the hotel room door beside her.

"What did you just do?" she asked.

"Shut down the security camera in the hallway for just a blip, long enough to hide our presence."

"So you can do that again for Ryker?"

"Maybe," he said cheerfully. "But Ryker is already in the room beside us."

Just then the connecting hotel door opened, and Ryker walked in. She frowned at him. "And how did you get here so fast?"

"You'd be surprised," he said. In his hands were large bags of food. "Chinese food for all."

She stared at him, looked at the food, and shook her head. "How? I don't know how," she said. "It doesn't matter. I'll enjoy the food regardless." She quickly emptied the bags, while the two men set up the electronics.

As soon as he was up and running, Asher walked over, snagged a large bowl from one of many, and started eating. He looked at her. "Eat," he said. "You need energy."

She nodded and picked up one of the rolls in a small container, then moved on to the next dish. Finally filled up, she sat off to the side.

ASHER COULD SEE the fatigue on her face, the worry and the unrest. There had to be a certain amount of disquiet just being in a scenario so different from her norm. "You doing okay?"

She nodded. "I'll be fine."

"It could get pretty hairy," he said.

"Got it," she said. "But I still don't understand how you plan on tracking down the twins."

"We're still figuring that out," he said. "The problem is, they can be anywhere. We need to locate the vehicle that we suspect took them out of here."

"But they stopped the videos at the same time, like you guys did?"

"Absolutely. But the city cameras are a different story. I doubt they shut all those down."

Her mouth formed an *O* as she stared at him in surprise; then she nodded. "Of course. A city like this, cameras are all over the place."

"Exactly," he said.

She went back to select more food, while he quickly devoured his.

"What's likely to be the twins' reaction when they wake up from something like this?"

"Panic," she said. "Crying, wailing, potentially sitting and rocking in place. Depends on how bad the circumstances are."

"So what's the easiest way to deal with them?"

She winced. "Honestly? Probably drugging them."

"That makes sense." He frowned, nodded, and asked, "Do they handle drugs well?"

She shrugged and said, "They have been on and off medications for years without any noticeable effects. But, if the kidnappers have a doctor with the twins, it'll probably be okay."

"Good," he said.

"So it'll take all three of us then to wrangle the twins?" Ryker asked. "Size and weight?" He looked at Mickie.

"The twins are five-eleven and 125 pounds. Very willowy and obviously very beautiful."

"Were there ever any security issues before?"

"Once," she said. "Somebody thought the twins shouldn't be modeling but should grace his house instead."

"And, of course, the twins didn't think much of that, did they?"

She shook her head. "I don't know the details. You should ask Chandra about that."

Immediately he picked up the phone and made the call. But Chandra was asleep, and the man who answered wouldn't wake her.

In a hard voice Asher said, "That's fine, but I want the details of a scenario that Mickie just mentioned. And I want answers in five minutes." Not believing that he'd get them, he quickly put Beau on it as well in the chat box again. That was the good thing about the chat window. Beau had men on the other end, so one person could be working on one request, and another could be working on the other. Beau came back fast.

They were escorted from a modeling shoot and taken to his house, where the Spanish-speaking owner wanted them to stay as his *guests*, Beau typed.

Kidnapped then?

Persuaded, Beau added. **No charges were ever pressed. He apologized profusely to Chandra and said that he was just bowled over by the twins' beauty.**

And yet, given their vulnerable state and position in society, Asher typed, **then** *persuasion* **is not exactly the right word.**

No. Chandra did let law enforcement in Spain know at the time, but this man was a wealthy patron, so it was all brushed under the carpet.

"I wonder if there's any chance that he's popped his head back up again?" Asher muttered. **Check out where he's at and what he's up to, please**, he typed in.

We have, and he's clear, safe at home and more interested in other *guests*.

At that, Asher refilled his bowl with noodles and quickly plowed through them. He loved Asian food at the best of times, but, when actually in China and getting the real thing, it was hard to not just sit here and take time to enjoy it. But it was time they didn't have.

Asher wanted a possible location to check out tonight, and he wanted it fast. Beau came back a few moments later and typed, **We picked up the white van heading toward one of the northern suburbs.**

Did you run down the license plate?

Yes, it's a rental. We got a facial match and have the two men's names.

The names didn't mean anything to Asher or Ryker or Mickie.

I'll pass it on to Chandra and ask if she knows them.

He quickly made that phone call. The guy who answered on the other end snapped, "She's still not awake. I still don't have the answer for you."

"Do you know these two men?" Asher rattled off their names.

"No," the guard said. "Who are they?"

"Potentially the driver and the passenger of the vehicle that carried away the twins."

The guard's breath sucked back tight against his throat.

Asher nodded on the other end. "Exactly. Now's the time to wake her." And he hung up.

CHAPTER 6

MICKIE SAT IN the corner; watching the men work was astonishing. They made phone calls, placed orders, mapped out routes, and basically tracked anything and everything they wanted in life. "Do you have unlimited permission to do this?"

Asher shot her a hard look. "You'd be grateful for this if you were the kidnappee."

"I know," she said quietly. "You're right. I never really expected to see this behind-the-scenes work. I've never seen you in action before."

He quirked his lips at her but stayed quiet.

Of course, she had seen him in action. Just a different kind of action. And he was just as good at that as he was here right now with this. Disturbed by the memory, she got up, walked around, noting two beds here and a connecting door. She walked to the connecting door and saw two more beds on the other side and asked, "Which bed is mine?"

"Take one on either side," Asher said. "We'll wake you if it's important."

She hesitated and asked, "But will you wake me if you leave?"

"I'll wake you if we both leave," he said as a half-measure. "Will that work?"

She frowned and then nodded. "I guess I don't need to

go with you on every field trip of yours, provided you don't think the twins will be at the end destination."

"We won't know that," he said.

"Then I need to come with you all the time," she said. "If the twins are drugged, it won't be too bad, but if they aren't … If you need things to happen quietly, then I better come with you."

"Do they care about you that much?"

"I don't know about that. But I'll be that balance, that rock that they need to latch on to," she said firmly. "And, as a nurse, I can also regulate their health coming out of a medicated state. I have some medications for them as well, not to mention insulin."

"We'll consider it," he said, and he dropped his gaze to the laptop again.

She hated that about him. He'd always had such an ability to detach from her and to focus on what was going on around him. Of course, it was ideal for the work he did. He was here to save the twins, and that's what she wanted first and foremost. She had no business complaining.

She just couldn't believe any of this crap about forcing Chandra to plan some woman's wedding. None of that part made any sense. And yet, who knew? She didn't like most people to begin with, and she certainly understood that some brides-to-be were absolute nightmares. But this? It sounded more like revenge, manipulation-control. As if this wasn't as much about the ransom money but more about getting a service. Like, a one-million-dollar rushed wedding for free and a five-million-dollar fine.

That just didn't sit right, but it was also just believable enough that they couldn't dismiss it. As she lay on the bed atop the covers and crossed her fingers over her belly, she wondered how Chandra was coping. Did her son know what was going on? Mickie had met him, but it hadn't been pleasant. Plus, she had been privy to a few moments watching him with the staff and even his relations.

He was the epitome of the rich condescending self-entitled male, feeling his patriarchal duty to ignore women, even megawealthy ones. Did he have anything to do with the twins? Did he care, or would he just close the door on this whole scenario? She half suspected that's what would happen. When her phone rang a few minutes later, she wasn't at all surprised to see it was Chandra.

"Have they found anything?"

"The vehicle that the twins *may* have been taken in," Mickie stressed. "Asher is tracking it online throughout Shanghai to a northern suburb."

"Why aren't they on the road after it already?" Chandra cried out.

"First off," Mickie said, "I'm not part of their inner workings. They will tell me when they have a plan, but, until then, they're still pulling all the pieces together. Second, they just arrived, Chandra. Give them some time."

"I don't think I like them," Chandra said, her voice tremulous.

"You don't have to like them," Mickie said gently. "You just must let them do their job."

"It's been almost two full days," Chandra snapped.

"I know," Mickie said. "I was there too. Remember?"

"I'm so sorry," Chandra said. "I never meant to put you in any danger. I didn't think something like this would happen. It's been so long since anything bad had happened. Who would have thought this?"

"Well, you need to give the men the details about what

happened before, when that man in Spain kidnapped the twins," Mickie said. "These men can't operate if they don't have all the information necessary."

"It was so long ago," she said sadly. "I hate to dredge it all up again."

"And what if it's the same guy? What if he's just waited for another opportunity to grab them again?"

"I doubt it," Chandra said. Then she groaned. "Fine. Put Asher on the phone, please?"

Mickie got up off the bed, walked into the other room, and held her phone out to Asher. "It's Chandra. She wants to talk to you."

At that point in time, she collapsed beside Ryker, who was busy working on his laptop. "You guys heading out tonight?" Mickie asked in a low voice.

"As soon as we can pinpoint a possible location of the twins, yes," he said. "Did you get any sleep?"

"No," she said. "My mind is too overwhelmed."

"Maybe," he said, "but you need to be aware and awake before we head out."

"How much longer do we have before we leave?"

"Well, we're hoping to be on the road no later than one a.m., to make the best use of the nighttime hours."

She groaned. "Fine. I'll head back and try to sleep."

Just then Asher finished the call and held up her phone. "You've got three hours, and then we're leaving."

And, with that, he went back to his laptop.

ASHER WAS READY at a quarter to nine. With the checks all done, and everything packed up and ready to go, he walked to the door between the two hotel rooms and studied her sleeping form. He wanted to leave her where she was, where she was safe, but he also knew that, if there was a problem with the twins, Mickie could be instrumental in keeping them quiet as he and Ryker got them safely away.

Seeing Mickie like this ... brought back so many memories. She always slept curled up in a tight ball. He used to wrap himself around her and hold her protectively at night.

Just then her sleepy voice whispered, "Is it time?"

And it was like an arrow to his groin. That same sleepy voice awash with dreams, and yet, soaked with sex appeal. He shook his head, trying to send everything out of his mind again. "Yes, it is," he said. "Time to go. Get dressed. We're leaving in five."

She threw back the bedcovers while he watched; then she got up and bolted into the bathroom. She wore just a T-shirt over her underclothes, and he knew that she'd be ready to go within a few minutes. He hated to even take her. He'd much rather leave her where she would be safe, and he wouldn't worry about watching out for her. He was hyperaware of her every movement. Something he hadn't expected.

But, if she would be of any help with the twins, then he would use her. The twins themselves could be in tough shape and might need medical attention. Maybe Mickie was right. If the twins saw her, they might calm down. It'd be easier to get them moved about. He didn't know what kind of reaction they would have in a dangerous situation. Some women couldn't stop freaking out and crying, and he'd been forced to knock them out in order to get them to safety. And others went along, silent and frozen, following orders like automatons—and not just the women. Men were the same.

While Asher waited at the connecting doorway, she

came out of the bathroom and quickly dressed, throwing her jeans on this time. She now had socks and sneakers on too. "Am I bringing my bags?" He hesitated. She nodded, picked up her purse that doubled as her medic bag, with all the valuables she had in it, and said, "If we come back, fine. Otherwise, there's nothing in my other bags I need. I'll keep this bag with me. I've already packed up enough for a few days."

He smiled at her, appreciating her understanding. "I don't know how fast we'll be moving."

"Understood," she said. She put the big tote purse over her shoulder and said, "Let's go."

He led the way out, and, instead of the elevator, they used the stairs and slipped all the way down to the ground floor. There, as they walked out toward the entrance, Ryker drove up beside them once again. She got in the back. "You guys move so quietly," she said as she stared out at the night. "It's like you live in some sort of shadowland."

"We do," Ryker said quietly. "Most of the work we do is in the dark."

She nodded.

They exited the hotel underground parking lot, moving at speeds she wouldn't normally be traveling, staring at the streetlights all around her.

Asher watched her face for a while, looking for some reaction, but she just seemed to be taking it all in. Finally he faced Ryker and asked, "Any update?"

"No," Ryker said. "We have what we have right now."

"Good," he said. "Let's go." They raced across town, but even Shanghai was busy at night. Not as bad as during the day, but plenty of people moved even now. Driving as fast as they could, they headed toward the GPS location Asher had on his laptop screen.

When the vehicle rolled to a stop, their destination was a small run-down house. Asher got out of the car, leaving Ryker and Mickie behind, and approached from the left. He walked all around the outside, doing a full check, and saw nothing except a single light on downstairs. The rest of the house was dark.

He returned to the car, quietly opened her car door, and murmured to Mickie, "Do the twins need to sleep with the lights on?"

"Yes," she said. She peered at the house beside them and said, "They always need one light left on."

"That's good to know," Ryker said.

"I'll check it out. You keep her here." Asher quietly closed the car door and disappeared down the block. He circled back around from the far side and then came up between the two houses. It was a country area with not too much in motion. A few dogs could be heard in the distance. The house in question was dark on the side, and a window was partially open; a car was in the driveway. He opened it, front and back, but it was empty. The house was next. He swooped around to the back and slipped inside the open window.

As he walked across the bare floor, he heard crying on the other side of a wall. And then a man saying, "Just shut up." Instead the sobbing continued. Asher frowned. A woman crying didn't mean it was one of the two he was looking for. And, if it was one of the twins, where was the other one?

He hadn't considered that the kidnappers would split them up. Surely that would make the twins harder to control. He quietly turned the knob and pulled the door open toward him. But the noises were deeper inside the house. He walked closer, knowing that he was trespassing on what could be a completely innocent husband-and-wife argument.

Asher heard the sound of a door slamming, and a man swearing and cussing in a language Asher didn't recognize. He quickly stepped into and around a corner and waited for the man to rush past him. As soon as he was upstairs, Asher swept through to the door and found it locked. He quickly unlocked it and pushed it open enough to stick his head around the corner. He found one woman, but not the one he expected. He bent down at her side. "Are you all right?"

She stared up at him and frowned. "Who are you?"

"I'm looking for the twins," he said.

She clapped a hand over her mouth and stared at him, her eyes wide.

He nodded. "Do you know where they are?" Her gaze went to the door, and he realized that she was likely terrified the other man would come back. "Are they here?"

She hesitated and then shook her head.

"Do you know where they are?"

She gave a tiny shrug of her shoulders.

He settled back and asked, "Are you a prisoner here?"

She nodded, and he asked, "Do you want your freedom?"

Instantly her head bobbed up and down.

He helped her to her feet and out the bedroom door, and then he lifted her up so she could escape through the window. He followed her outside. As soon as they were free and clear, several houses away, he asked, "Do you know anything about the twins?"

"That's why he's angry at me," she whispered. "I'm a

nurse's aide, and one of them was having a bad attack, but I didn't know what was wrong."

"Did they take the twins away from here?"

She nodded. "To a private hospital. But I don't know if they're still there now."

"Are the twins okay?"

"I don't know," she admitted. "I think one, maybe both, had a diabetic low."

"Do you know where the private hospital is?" he asked. "I'm here on their mother's request."

Her jaw dropped in an instant. "Really?" She looked back at the house. "I don't know anything about that."

"They were kidnapped, and the mother is being blackmailed," he snapped. "I need details." He ushered her across the road to the car. He quickly pushed her into the back seat beside Mickie. When he got in, he turned and said, "She was looking after the twins until one had a bad attack."

The woman started to cry. "I didn't know she was diabetic."

Mickie cried out, "Oh, my God, I recognize you. You were at the hotel."

The woman looked at her, her lips trembling as she nodded.

"So, you were part of the plot to kidnap the twins?" Asher asked.

She stared at him in fear.

He watched as Mickie grasped the woman's hands and said, "It's okay. But we need to find them."

"I told him that the men took the twins to a hospital."

"Which one?" Mickie asked urgently.

"A private one," she said. "One where they deal with special patients."

"Got it," Ryker said. "But which one?"

The woman took a deep breath. "Not far from here."

"Do you know the way?" Asher snapped.

The woman nodded. "Please, can we leave?"

At that, Ryker took off and headed back onto the street. "Which way?"

She did her best to direct them, got lost once, and then finally they drove past a more institutionalized-looking building, but it was older and more run-down.

"It doesn't look very high-tech," Asher said.

"It doesn't," she said. "But they will look after the twins."

"Do you think they're still there?"

"I don't know," she said. "The men were looking to move them."

"Where to?"

The woman didn't know.

Asher sagged in place. "What were you being paid to look after them?"

"Sorry?" She didn't appear to understand the question.

"He wants to know why you were involved in their kid-napping," Mickie repeated.

"I wasn't," she said. "They asked me to look after them. I didn't know that the twins were held against their will."

"What kind of condition were they in?" Mickie asked not believing a word she said.

"They wouldn't stop crying once they woke up from the drugs. It just never stopped," she said.

"Of course not," Asher said.

Mickie reached out and said, "Can you please tell me a little more? I look after them. I'm really worried about them."

"I don't think the men were prepared for their condition," the woman muttered. "I was kind of an afterthought."

"But, by then, Alisha had already slid into a diabetic coma, I presume," Mickie said.

The woman nodded. "Yes, and then the men took her away."

"One or both?" Asher asked.

"Both," she said, "but it was the day before yesterday."

"So, just after they were kidnapped?"

"Eight to ten hours afterward," she said.

"Do you know if they're okay? Have you heard the kidnappers talk about their condition at all?" Mickie asked.

"No," she said. "I just wanted to be released, and they wouldn't let me free."

"Were they expecting you to stay and look after the women when they brought them back?"

"I think so. But they were also angry because I couldn't fix what was wrong in the first place," she said.

As they pulled up to the side of the hospital, she looked at the building and said, "That's not a very nice place either."

"What do you mean?" Ryker said.

"It's a place where, if you have money, you can put people away."

"So, they're keeping them there. Interesting," Asher said. "I guess you can't keep people prisoner anymore at too many places, particularly if they need medical care?"

"No," she said. "A lot of places are in town, but it's the medical care that you need here."

"And how come you speak such good English?" Mickie asked.

"I spent a lot of time in Europe," the woman said. "I went to school in the US too."

"We want the names of the men who kidnapped the twins," Ryker said.

"Not only that," Asher said, "we need to know everything you know about the kidnapping. Is there any chance that the twins have already been removed from this hospital?"

"It's possible," she said. "The men were looking for a short-term solution before they moved them again."

"Move them where?" Mickie asked urgently. "I need to get to them."

She looked back at Mickie. "Are you Mickie?"

Mickie nodded, tears coming to her eyes. "Yes, I am."

CHAPTER 7

"T HE TWINS WANT you," the woman said. "They kept crying out for you."

She couldn't believe that the twins had used her name. Mickie nodded and wiped the tears from the corner of her eyes. "They must be terrified."

"Very. Almost uncontrollable," the woman said. "The men weren't expecting that."

Mickie sat back. "How could they not be? They're autistic. They need special care. They need a full-time caregiver."

"For some reason, the men thought they'd be quiet and would not be difficult."

Mickie snorted at that. "The twins are notoriously difficult. They need a place where they can be together."

"Shit," Ryker said. He looked at Asher. "My turn." And he exited the vehicle and disappeared.

Mickie leaned forward. "Where's he going?"

"To see if he can find any information on the twins," Asher said. He was already on his phone and had the laptop up with a chat window.

"What are you doing?"

"Tracking down the two men who kidnapped the twins and to get a history on this place. If the twins are in there, we need to know where."

"Chances are they've been moved again," the woman

said. "I'm not sure what the deal was, but the men didn't want to keep them at the hospital for long."

"Because of the cost or because someone might recognize the twins?" Mickie asked.

"I don't know," she said, but she didn't elaborate.

Mickie wasn't sure she trusted her at all either. Mickie understood that she'd been locked up and that Asher had rescued her. But that didn't mean that she was willing to share very much about what was going on. "What else can you tell us?" Mickie asked.

The woman shrugged. "I know that a lot of money is involved," she said.

"And were you expecting to get some of it?"

The woman shook her head. "No, I was paid to look after the twins. No extra money was coming for me. And they won't pay me now."

"Just as well," Mickie said. "These twins were kidnapped. And that won't go well for anybody involved in their kidnapping."

At that, the woman stared at her in horror. "I had nothing to do with that. I was just hired to look after them."

"Well, you didn't do it very well, did you?" Asher snapped. "And neither are you making it easy for us to help the twins."

"I don't know anything," she cried out. "You can't blame this on me."

"Maybe not," Asher said. "But, if you don't start talking, it's not like you'll get a lighter sentence."

At that, the woman shut up and curled into the corner.

Mickie turned to Asher. "That's not helping."

He raised an eyebrow at her.

She groaned. "Look," she said, turning to the woman.

"We need to get the twins before they crash again."

"That's why they were in the hospital," the woman said patiently. "It's why the men are mad at me."

"Do you know the men?"

She shrugged and said, "Somewhat."

"Is one your boyfriend? Family?" At that, Asher leaned and twisted around farther, so he could study the woman's face. "One is your brother, isn't he?"

Her gaze went flat.

He nodded. "So, you're in this up to your eyeballs. You were expecting money from this. Were you really locked in that room, or was that just a trick too?"

"I told you," she said. "They're upset with me because I couldn't help the twins."

"Well, guess what?" he said. "If anything happens to the twins, it's on your head now too. We're calling for a pickup for you."

"What do you mean, *a pickup?*" the woman cried out, frightened.

"Well, you don't get to walk away now," he said. "You were involved in an international kidnapping incident, and that's not pretty jail time."

Just then Ryker slipped back into the car. He turned on the engine and drove away.

"What did you find out?"

"They were moved earlier this morning," he said. "About an hour and a half ago."

Asher twisted around to look at the woman and said, "And you knew about that?"

She was silent and sagged into the corner of the back seat.

"Well, obviously you know more than you're telling us,"

Mickie said, glaring at her. "In that case, just dump her at the police station. They will lock her up. And throw away the key. In a place like this, nobody'll care about her."

"No," the woman cried out in terror.

"Yes," Mickie said. "You could tell us more. But instead, you didn't give a damn about the twins that you were helping to keep prisoner. In that case, we won't help you either."

"Look. I can tell you," she said, "but I'll get in trouble."

"You're *already* in trouble," Asher said.

She thought about it for a nanosecond; then she said, "They're moving them to the docks."

"And why would we believe you now?" Asher asked.

"I'm telling you the truth."

"And why are they taking them to the docks?"

"They'll take them to a ship and hold them in the harbor," she said. "They figured they'd have less chance of being seen."

"What kind of a ship?"

The woman shrugged. "I think it's a fishing boat."

"Well, that makes sense," Ryker said. "A million of them are out here."

"Exactly," the woman said. "But they were looking for medication to knock them out because they were being so noisy. They figured, if the twins were on a ship, nobody would hear them."

Mickie thought about that and then nodded. "Unfortunately she's quite right."

"Is that the only way to keep them happy?"

"No, not the only way," Mickie said. "But it's probably the easiest way in these circumstances. The twins are unhappy, and they want to go home. They don't understand what's happening, and they are scared."

"No one will hear them out on the water," Ryker said calmly.

"Damn," Asher said. "I just came from the harbor."

"Different harbor," Ryker said with a laugh.

"True," Asher said. "But, if it's a fishing vessel, hundreds of them are out there, if not thousands."

"They're going up the coastline a little bit," the woman said.

"Until how long?"

"Until they're contacted," the sister said. "There's money to be paid. They won't hand the twins over, until they get paid."

"And who's *they?*"

"My brothers," she admitted grudgingly. "But they kidnapped the twins at somebody else's orders."

"Whose orders?"

She shook her head. "I don't know. I just know that they were hired to do the job."

"And was anybody else hired?"

Fear whispered across her face again. "Yes," she said. "Two other men to help. And they're both dead."

She clammed up then and wouldn't say any more.

They handed off the woman to the local authorities shortly thereafter and promptly updated Beau.

THEY PULLED UP to a restaurant that looked like more of an internet café. Asher needed a cup of coffee and a chance to sort out where in the harbor this fishing boat had gone. Chinese flowed in a steady stream of conversation around him, dotted by bits of English. More people spoke English than he expected. He was no sooner sitting at the table in the back, away from the other customers, with Mickie beside him and Ryker across from him, when the chat window popped up on his phone. It told them to call. He quickly made the call and listened as information was passed along, but it was old information he already knew. "I need to know where the boat is," he said.

"I hear you," Beau said. "Neither of the brothers have a boat registered to them."

"Friends? Family?"

"Or the sister?" Ryker asked from across the table.

Asher nodded. "Check the sister's friend circle too. The twins are on a boat in the harbor somewhere."

Beau said, "Hold on the line while I check that out."

"What about satellite imagery?" Mickie asked beside him. He shot her a look. She shrugged. "Just trying to help."

"Satellite imagery is something we're working on, but we've got a lot of boats leaving the harbor today."

"Sure," she said. "But maybe you can check with the port itself to see if anybody saw the twins while they were loaded onto the boat."

"Chances are they wouldn't have gone to the port at all but someplace off to the side and out of the way," Ryker added. "You know all kinds of nooks and crannies are to be found for a boat to hide while the men move the twins out."

"Well, there has to be some way to find them," Asher said in exasperation. While he watched, Ryker quickly went to the counter and ordered them food and drinks. Asher settled against the wall and watched the busy café around him. "We're running out of time," he said to Beau, still holding. "We found one location, but we need to find the next one."

"Did the hospital give you any other information?" Beau asked.

"No," Asher said. "Once we realized the twins had been moved already, there didn't seem to be much point. I didn't want to raise any alarms in case those men had connections there."

"Good point," Beau said. "Give us a couple hours on this."

"Well, that's all the time you've got," he said, already setting an alarm on his watch. "What about the harbormaster? Do they keep track of fishing boats?"

"No, not small crafts," Beau said, "which is why it's an ideal location to keep the twins."

"But not long-term," Asher said. "There are basics to consider, like medicine and hygiene."

"That's really not a top priority in this location," Beau said.

"I know," Asher said. "But it is something that we must consider."

"I know."

He hung up at that, opened up his laptop, and started searching. Then he brought up the chat box once more and typed **Give me the satellite feeds of the harbor.**

Almost immediately he got a link. He quickly searched through them, and he was right. Probably two to three hundred fishing boats moved in and around through the satellite feed. He started early the night before, but, with night satellite images, you didn't get to see much, especially if the kidnappers' boat had gone out without any lights.

Most of them didn't have any lights at all and were very hard to track. He backtracked the feeds about six hours earlier and kept going through them. The trouble was, there were too many boats to track. Without identifying numbers, it was impossible to move from one feed to the other and to keep any semblance of order. Swearing under his breath, he moved up the coastline, hoping that maybe he'd have a better visual. But that didn't help either.

The chat window opened up. **The sister's boyfriend has a boat.**

Where is it now?

In the harbor.

Is it empty?

Believed to be, yes.

How big?

Too small.

So how does that help us?

The older brother has friends with boats.

Possible. I still don't have any idea where up the coast they are though, Asher typed. **I'm checking the feeds but there are literally hundreds of boats.**

I know. Same problem here.

He frowned and typed, **On the off chance, does Chandra's son own a boat?**

He owns several, but none are in this part of the world.

Interesting.

Asher settled back as plates of food arrived, checking his countdown timer for Beau to get back with him. Asher quickly served himself, his mind moving at a rapid pace as he contemplated his newest theory. Just because somebody had a boat didn't make them guilty of kidnapping and holding somebody against their will. The fact that somebody owned a boat meant that they were quite comfortable on the water most likely. And that brought up a whole different concept.

Commercial fishing boats around?

Dozens at any given hour.

He winced at that. Of course. He headed back to his feeds, studying some of the bigger fishing boats as they came and went. He checked back. **Any logs for particular companies?**

All companies keep logs.

Okay, so anybody not come back last night?

Checking.

Asher went back to his feed, studying fishing boats moving farther up the coastline. Somebody here had to know something. He slogged through this for about thirty minutes before the chat box popped up again. **Notoriety Express had four boats out overnight.**

What locations?

He was quickly given their respective GPS locations.

Do they keep track of the boats all day?

Yes.

Any up the coast?

Two.

Big enough?

Yes.

Anything suspicious about their activity?

No.

Keep checking with other companies.

There had to be dozens of companies. Not everybody would be fishing in the same area, but it's possible that some of these people might have seen something. But getting anybody to volunteer information was a whole different story. Swearing, he closed the lid to his laptop and returned to his food.

Ryker looked over and said, "It'll be hard to track down a single fishing boat, especially if family owned and unmarked and without running lights."

"Harder than I thought, yes," Asher said quietly. "Which makes it a very good cover on the kidnappers' part."

"So, instead of tracking the boat, why don't we track the men?" Mickie said.

He glanced at her and said, "That's in progress."

"Sure," she said, "but they must have connections."

"We haven't found anybody with a boat connected to them. The sister that we dumped off with the authorities, her boyfriend has a boat, but it's too small and still in place."

"But the men must work? Or was this a private job?"

"They were hired," he said.

"So who hired them? How did they contact them?"

He stared at her, sighing audibly.

She shrugged. "I get it. You're on it."

"Yes, we're on it," he said. "But answers are few and far between."

"I know," she said, slumping in her chair. "I'm just frustrated."

"Understandable," he said.

"You guys want a refill on drinks?" When both nodded, she hopped up, asked at the counter for a full carafe of coffee and another of ice water. Asher smiled at her as she placed them on their table, a waitress behind her with a platter carrying cream and sugar, spoons, and clean coffee cups and water glasses.

"Thank you both," Asher said to Mickie and the waitress, before she smiled and took off. Asher glanced at Ryker. "I wonder if the bank accounts would help."

"I'll find out," Ryker said, as he started working on his laptop.

"You can't really get into people's bank accounts, can

you?"

Asher gave another sigh of frustration.

"Like you said, we need answers." She immediately zipped her mouth closed and settled back into her chair. Eventually she lay her head on her arms and dozed off.

Meanwhile, Ryker worked on the bank accounts and the method of payment to the kidnappers, which in Asher's mind would likely be cash, considering where they were, and Asher kept working on the boats. The trouble was, so many people owned fishing boats in a place like this, probably make their living that way. And the boat didn't even have to be terribly fancy, it just needed to be big enough to hold three people.

If both of the twins were unconscious, that was even easier. Not to mention the fact that the kidnappers may have taken the twins up the coastline, but that didn't mean they didn't move them onto land when they got there. Or that they were shipped from here onto land. Asher went back to the hospital's location and checked the feeds. If they couldn't track the kidnappers on water, then he had to get back to ground zero and track them from there.

And forty more mind-numbing minutes of sifting through satellite feeds, that's when he, just by accident, caught sight of the van exiting the hospital on the feed. He slowed down and realized it pulled in behind two others. But that one was the one he had been looking for. He slowly tracked it as far as he could, picking up different cameras and watching it disappear and then reappearing online as it headed north. He frowned as it did a series of turns. He lost it several times and then found it again as the traffic cameras picked it up. Once located again, the van headed onto the main freeway and moved up along the coastline.

"Doesn't look like they found a fishing boat in town," he said. "They're moving north."

"Which makes sense," Ryker said. "They need to keep those famous faces hidden."

"I wonder if they knew that that would be the more challenging part of this job."

"They probably didn't think about it."

"And yet," Asher added, "the medical angle may be the hardest part. The kidnappers just have to hide the models to avoid them being recognized. And—like Mickie has said—they want to be home, alone, in the garden. But their recurring medical issues—the diabetes, the stomach ailments, plus dealing with their autism—must require a lot of time each and every day. Not to mention the money needed to treat these two. I don't think the five-million-dollar ransom is their final demand."

Asher knew what Ryker meant because every job had one surprising aspect. Even though you considered as many angles as you could think of, there always seemed to be something that you couldn't quite envision or control. And, in this case, it was the twins' famous faces. But then, how famous? Particularly over here. "Got them heading toward a small—smaller," he corrected, "town."

"You mean, a village?"

"Well, he's getting off the freeway and going through a village," he said. "But now I've lost the cameras." He swore softly and checked through the time stamp but found nothing afterward. He quickly switched over to the satellite feed and checked for the time stamp that he had backtracked to see if the vehicle showed up anywhere.

"Too bad we can't get real-time on some of this stuff," Ryker muttered.

"Check and see if you can," Asher said. "I'm still trying to track the vehicle once it left the freeway, but the satellite feed isn't helping."

"Which just means that either they got off the main road or the feed itself is in the wrong time stamp."

Asher checked the date and the time and quickly back-tracked a little bit more, and, sure enough, he found something resembling the van. But, from the satellite feed, it was not anywhere near as clear as he needed that van to be. The local cameras were much clearer. But the satellite feed was his best bet, so he followed it as far as he could, until they pulled into a small parking spot along the edge of a marina. He watched as one man got out and, moving at a fast pace, headed toward a boat moored at the side. But, instead of unloading anybody from the back of the vehicle, he hopped onto the boat and took off, heading up north again. "Well, he didn't get anybody out of that vehicle," he whispered.

"Could be meeting somebody," Ryker said.

"In what way?" But just as he asked, Asher watched the small boat picking up and meeting with a slightly larger one. He pulled up beside it, and the two men had a conversation, and then both boats headed back. As he watched, the two of them tied up the boat, and one hopped out and returned to the van. The man from the other boat came with him. And very quickly, two people were moved from the back of the van into the bigger boat. "Gotcha," he whispered softly.

Immediately Ryker got up from the table and came around to take a look at Asher's laptop screen and nodded. "Well, that's the vessel. But how do we identify it from any other?"

At that point in time, the satellite feed got glitchy, which was so common unfortunately. He tried to adjust the settings, but it blacked out for a moment. When it came back on again, it was for a completely different time on the same day. And, of course, the boat was long gone. Asher swore again. He quickly backtracked it to where he got the last visual. He came in as close as he could and took several screen shots of the vessel as well as of this van, but they were blurry, and he knew it wouldn't help much. "At least we know this boat is somehow connected to the drivers, and the boat guy knew the other guys. He headed out, met up with them, and brought them in."

"What we need is a way to track the fishing boat now," Ryker said. "Try running that satellite feed through a different optimizer. It might give you a few more pixels. Likely broken up, but who knows."

Because the satellites rotated around the world, they would have to shift from one satellite to another to continue monitoring a fixed location. Asher quickly ran the link through another program and dumped it into the chat window. Then he explained where he needed the missing minutes.

The waitress came by, switching out their empty carafes for two more full ones. Mickie woke up, gave her a sleepy smile and said a quick "Thank you," as the waitress left.

The answer came back quickly. **You mean missing hours?**

Whatever. I need to know where this boat went from there.

And he sent them the last-known feed with the time stamp.

After that, feeling slightly better but frustrated to have lost it yet again, he saw still more food remained and realized that his appetite was in no way appeased. He quickly refilled his plate, looking to see if the others were eating. "Anything on your end?" he asked Ryker.

"Yes. Lump sums paid into a special account under one brother's name."

"What about the other brother?"

"No," he said.

"Interesting. I wonder if the unpaid brother is aware that his brother is getting this money."

"It's possible. It's hard to say though."

"Maybe," Mickie said quietly. "But it would be good ammo when we get them together."

"Right," said Asher. "It's easier to pit brother A against brother B and see what comes up."

"They could be sharing it, or the brother could be paid for something else?"

"True enough. Any withdrawals against it?"

"Two," he said. "And decent amounts."

"Possibly paying for the boat, possibly paying for the hospital."

"Could be both," he said. "Could be paying for his brother too."

"What kind of a percentage against the whole amount?"

Ryker shrugged. "Negligible. We're talking about fifteen hundred out of the whole fifty thousand."

"Interesting," Asher said. "Definitely something we need to follow up on. Any way to check where the money came from?"

"Working on it now but it's gone through a couple international banks."

"So, not from Shanghai itself?"

"No, not a local bank."

"Interesting again."

"Find the son's bank accounts to see if he has any transactions overseas," Mickie suggested.

"He does a lot of business, so he will," Ryker said.

"If he's involved, surely he's smart enough not to run any of this through his business accounts," Asher said. "Much better to have done it personally, via cash or a fake ID, and keep audits out of there. So I doubt that money trail will lead directly to him."

"I agree. Much better to have done cash," Ryker said.

"And that is quite possible. Pay somebody cash to run it through their account." He frowned, thinking about it. "We still don't have any motive though."

"No," Mickie said. "And I hope you're wrong about it being the twins' brother."

"I'm not saying it is their brother," Asher stated, as he plowed through his food. "What I am saying is that the brother is a suspect."

"But then you might as well make the mother a suspect too," Mickie said in astonishment.

He froze, turned to look at her, and asked, "Why?"

Mickie settled into her chair, as if to explain a long story, and then ended up saying, "It's a bit convoluted, but she gave the twins away at one point in time. Sometimes I think she'd be happier without them."

"Now that's a very interesting take," Asher said. "When I met her, she seemed extremely concerned about her daughters' whereabouts." He studied Mickie's face. "Was there ever any sign that she didn't want anything to do with them?"

"I mean, outside of the fact that she was never at home and that she was always traveling and that they never went anywhere with her, and then, out of the blue, this trip happens?"

"Oh," Ryker said. "That brings up a very interesting possibility too."

"But there are a lot easier ways to get rid of them," he said.

"And what are we talking about? *Getting rid of*," Mickie cried out. "The twins are lovely people. Nobody should be just tossing them away like garbage."

"When it comes to kidnapping," Asher said, his tone low, "if ransom isn't paid on time, which in this case is due in five days, or, if any of the other demands are not met, that's when the twins *do* become garbage."

Mickie's eyes widened, and she swallowed hard.

He could see her fingers clenched tightly together in her lap.

She nodded slowly and said, "I hope that never happens. Even though the twins have some issues, it's not fair. They're lovely people, and they deserve to have a happy life."

"Nothing about this is fair," Asher said. He put down his fork again, his fingers thrumming on the table. "So, now we've got the mother and the brother." He again checked his watch.

"Together, do you think?" Ryker asked.

Asher shook his head. "I highly doubt it. But then again, why would they bother with all this? The twins could just be committed somewhere in a home, where they'd be happy. The mother has enough money that that would be a negligible expense."

"Yes and no," Mickie said. "The twins are quite wealthy."

"So then, their own money could go toward their own

medical care and housing," Asher said. "Unless you know something we don't know."

"Possibly," she said. "The twins have not just their own money but their grandmother's money that was left for their care."

"How much?"

She winced. "A lot."

"We're talking superwealthy people here already," Asher said. "What's *a lot?*"

"I think $140 million," she said, as she consolidated some of their dirty plates together and set them on the empty table beside them. Then she gathered their trash and placed it all atop the plates. When she sat down again, she noted that both men had stopped to stare at her.

"Great," Asher said. "That's enough for mass murder."

"Again this is too convoluted," Ryker said. "Much easier to just lock the twins away. That money shouldn't be accessed by them. Somebody's looking after it, like a trustee or a guardian or even some bank executive or an attorney. The twins won't have guardianship on their own. Somebody has guardianship over them."

"Chandra does. But she can't touch that money."

"How do you know?"

"I saw some paperwork Chandra was trying to talk to the twins about."

"Do you know what it was?"

"Chandra was pretty frustrated. It was about investing their money to make more money, I think."

"Sounds like something we might need to take a look at," Asher said.

Ryker cracked his knuckles and said, "That's my kind of thing. I'm on it."

"It's not like you can get a copy of it," Mickie said.

"Maybe not," he said. "But I can certainly find out what lawyer is dealing with this. And just what those documents were."

"He won't talk to you," Mickie said. "Why would he? Chandra is his client, and so are the twins and likely the brother. That's confidential."

"Well, if I was the brother," Asher said, "I would certainly have a different lawyer. Particularly if I didn't get along with my mom or my sisters."

"But that's you," Mickie said. "In my case, I'd have the same lawyer so the lawyer understood the family dynamics."

"But then he can't back one versus the other," Asher said. "And, if the brother is involved or is trying to separate ways, he needs someone on his side, not on the family's side."

CHAPTER 8

T HE INTERNET CAFÉ had a few more customers now, but the three of them were undisturbed.

Mickie didn't think Chandra could possibly be involved, but Mickie had certainly seen enough frustration on the mother's part when dealing with the twins and could understand that maybe Chandra had the odd wish to change the situation. The twins would need a lifetime of care, but the money was there for them. There was no need to go through this elaborate ruse. "It would make more sense if it was a competitor," she said.

"Why? Her reputation is much greater than an event like this," Asher said. "This is more likely about sympathy."

"What would that do for her?"

"Make her even more in demand than normal," Ryker said. "Except she's already in demand."

"And thinking of downsizing," Mickie added.

"But we only have her word on that," Asher said, studying Ryker's face. "Maybe do a check into that. See if we can get into her schedule and confirm that she is actually booked out four to five years."

Ryker nodded. "I guess the question is, if her business isn't so good, and she's not quite ready to retire, would this help bring in more business?"

"I don't understand why it'll bring in more," Mickie

said. "Nobody, including the media, is allowed to know about it."

"Until it's all solved," Asher said, "so it could be a big publicity stunt."

That was like a blow to her gut. She stared at him in shock. "Chandra is not like that. Besides, the twins have lots of money. Surely Chandra could access it, if she needed to, right?"

"For some people, who crave attention and success, pulling a kidnapping as a publicity stunt would be the worst thing for them. It would mean failure," he said with some spirit. "I would hope not, considering these are her own children, and they have special needs as well. But I have seen a lot of cases where the parents have done much worse."

She swallowed hard. "I'm pretty sure I don't like the world that you normally live in."

"No," he said. "I'm pretty sure you wouldn't."

"I guess it makes sense why we never stayed together."

At that, Ryker lifted his head and looked at the two of them. "Uh-oh."

Asher waved his hand at him. "It was a long time ago."

"Still …" Ryker continued.

"No *still*," Asher said. "She broke up with me, before I became a SEAL." He turned back to her.

She could see almost a reinforced blank look in his eyes.

"I don't understand what you are saying."

She shrugged. "It doesn't matter. I just don't think I would have liked to stick around you while you were learning to do all this."

"You didn't stick around for anything," he said, his voice harsh.

Mickie winced, realizing this had gotten a whole lot

more personal a whole lot faster than she had expected. "That's not what I meant."

He had already turned away, working on his laptop. She took a deep breath to try again and then realized there was really no point. She wasn't even sure how to explain where her mind had been when she had said that. And none of it should matter. It had been ten years ago.

Regardless, she still didn't want to believe that Chandra had anything to do with this kidnapping of her twins.

"She does have a very aggressive marketer," she said out of the blue. "I forgot about that. His name is Wilson Chang. I think Chandra's son, Edward, might have known him, but I'm not sure. Remember now, I'm not part of the inner circle. This is only what I've gleaned from being with the twins. And the sisters did talk a lot sometimes," she admitted.

"And you think Chang could be involved?"

"No, not necessarily. But, if you're correct, and he's ensuring that she stays in business, I guess that's one very twisted way of doing it."

"Possibly, but it's also possible that she *is* looking to cut back on the traveling and heading toward retirement."

"But we also must consider that," Mickie continued, "just because she's retiring, it doesn't mean that this Wilson Chang is ready to retire."

They stared at her, then started tapping away on their laptops.

She watched in amazement as these men accessed things that she didn't think any public servant or any government employee anywhere in the world were allowed to access. Surely this was just what hackers of the Dark Web could do? But as she watched one man slide through bank accounts and the other man slide through encrypted satellite feeds, backtracking and tracking down somebody in a vehicle, it just blew her away to consider that this was even possible.

The other thing that surprised her was to see Ryker and Asher, these action-oriented alpha males, tied to their laptops for almost three hours. Her butt was getting numb and she need to move. She didn't know how these guys went from extreme action to ... this stagnation.

She wasn't hungry as she'd eaten one plateful already, but the food just sat here, reminding her that she may not get another meal for a while. Deciding that she was better off tanking up a little bit first, she quickly shoveled a second portion onto her plate and looked up to see Asher watching her approvingly. She shrugged. "I don't know when the next opportunity will present itself," she said.

He nodded. "Exactly. Right now it's there. Who's to say beyond this?" He glanced at his watch.

"It's kind of depressing." She ate slowly as she watched the men plot their next course. The fact that they found a feed that showed the twins being moved onto a boat was huge. But it wasn't terribly helpful if they couldn't confirm where that boat was right now. The fact was, they were going through the mother's and the brother's businesses and bank accounts and then investigating the marketing manager, which maybe was her fault because she's the one who brought him up.

But how that would impact Asher's and Ryker's view of the sisters was downright disheartening. Mickie really wasn't an idealist, but she certainly believed in the sacrament of marriage and families. If the mother and the brother were involved in this kidnapping of the twins, that was just heartbreaking. The twins were very special. Amelia and

Alisha were both unique in their own way, and, at thirty now, they'd become a little more stubborn and set in their ways.

Mickie knew that all the twins wanted was to be home in their garden, and, after this, no way would they ever leave home again. And that just brought Mickie back to Chandra's reasoning for taking them on this trip. She had said that it would be one of the last times to travel to Asia, but the twins didn't really understand or know or care. They'd wanted their mother a long time ago, but she'd been too busy.

And maybe that was a harsh judgment on Mickie's part because it was so much easier to look at somebody else's wrongdoings and see them for what they were but not really understand how hard it must have been for Chandra to deal with her daughters. They must have been quite the handful growing up, and even the brother must hold a lot of resentment. He'd had nothing to do with them at the time that the twins had been in their lives, so Mickie couldn't imagine that he cared a whole lot now.

Yet, Edward was wealthy in his own right with his own businesses. He didn't need their money. He didn't need them in his life. But neither did he likely care enough to get rid of them. Who would? That was way too much effort, and the penalty of getting caught would be horrific. He'd be giving up everything in his life. Mickie doubted Edward cared that much. But it was so hard to judge since she didn't *know* him at all. It just brought up some terrible thoughts, and she didn't like that either. She muttered, "I hope you're wrong."

"I hope we are too," he said, "but we must be right enough here that we can get back on track."

"You've only been in town a few hours," she joked.

"And the twins might not have a few more hours."

She froze. Then she leaned forward and asked, "You don't really think they'll kill them, do you?"

"No, unless whatever is going on here doesn't come to completion fast enough, at which point the twins become a liability. Who'll look after them? They can't stay drugged for the rest of their life."

At that, Ryker lifted his head. "You know what?" he said. "That hospital. I think I need to check into that more."

"Why is that?"

"Because that would be a place to keep them for a long time."

"But obviously they didn't keep them there," Asher said patiently. "So why would they go back now?"

"Or they just made it look like the twins were leaving."

Asher sat back against his chair and stared at him. "It did look like it was them," he said cautiously, his face twisting on that idea.

"And most likely it was," Ryker said. "So then why would they take the chance of moving them again, if they were already at a hospital where they can get medical care?"

"Either visibility," he said, thinking about it, "or money."

Mickie nodded. "My vote is on money."

Asher turned to look at her. "Yet, what other reason would there be?"

"Those institutions want too much information," she said promptly. "With an intake of a patient in a legitimate place like that, the hospital administrators will possess certain information, and they also become the guardians of related medical files, etcetera."

"But wouldn't enough money make all that go away?"

"Yes, so we're back again to the money issue."

He nodded. "But if they don't have any other option long-term …"

"So, this is a temporary measure," Ryker said. "They potentially left the door open, so they could bring the twins back, if they need to."

"More likely they're probably keeping that as a last resort and hoping to find another place that's cheaper," she said. "All they would really need is a private nurse. And maybe a doctor to come by every once in a while."

"Even a private nurse probably isn't required," Ryker said. "If somebody had decent medical training—like a medic in the military—and if the twins were already hooked up to an IV, and their drugs were just injected into the bag, that's not exactly an issue."

She winced. "I really hate when you bring up the thoughts from the underbelly of life."

"I'm sure that they could be sold for body parts too," Ryker said, "if you want to go in that direction."

She swallowed hard. "In which case, then I'm sure there'll be several people who would want to buy the girls just for the sex trade."

"Except for their obvious difficulties," Ryker said.

"Do men care?" she asked bitterly. "If the traffickers can keep them drugged, people can use them and not have any worries." She looked up to see compassion in his face. She shrugged. "I know I'm really going off the rails here, but it hurts to consider that people don't look at them as people but as an *it*."

"They're definitely people with their own personalities," Ryker said. "But, when dealing with the underbelly of society, we must consider the worst-case scenario."

"And you're thinking death?" she asked.

Ryker's eyebrows popped up; he tilted his head, and he nodded.

"I would think being drugged for the rest of their life and used as somebody's toy would be worse," she said. "But that's just me."

"Well, I highly doubt that's what'll happen. They would be too difficult for that," Ryker said. "So, let's stick to the probabilities and not just possibilities."

She liked that about Ryker. He was very much of a *get to it* kind of person.

Asher appeared to be chafing though because he couldn't find what he needed to find.

"I guess there's no point in going to that area and finding out who might possibly know where the boat was?" Mickie offered.

"It would take more money," Asher said, "but I am considering just that."

"It's not too far away," Ryker said.

"No," Asher said. "But I don't want to waste time if we don't have to." He checked his watch again. "Our people have less than five minutes."

The waitress was kind enough to swap out their coffee and water carafes and also took away their dirty plates without interrupting them.

Just then the chat popped up. **We found a few things.** And sent pop-up links.

Asher quickly opened up the links, and, in one, he whistled.

Ryker immediately hopped up, came around, pulled a chair closer, and looked over his shoulder. "What are we looking at?"

"The brother's business enterprises. And the bottom line is, he's in the red."

"And could really use an infusion of cash," Ryker said.

"Sure," she said beside them. "But that's just business as usual. So many of them run in the red."

"But this is millions and millions. Eighty million to be exact."

She sat back and shook her head. "It's hard to even comprehend that much money period, but to imagine owing that much? How is it he got into so much trouble?"

"Building commercial properties. He's a developer, and one of his projects had some engineering failures, and a lot of the investors pulled out and left him covering most of the expenses."

"Is it back on track?"

He nodded. "As I read this, it appears that the project is moving forward, and he's trying to hang on to get it to the completion date."

"But something that size ..."

"It's a multiprong complex with a mall as the commercial space on the bottom floor and then residential areas on the towers above," he said. "So, eighty million is a normal price tag for that size building."

"If you say so." She shrugged. "And obviously he might *want* to use his sisters' money if he had some way to get to it, but I don't think anybody in business would use their own money to plug a hole like that."

"No, they usually grab another investor," Ryker said.

"But, regardless, Edward cannot access his sisters' money."

Ryker got up and paced the café as he did several stretches. When he was done, he asked, "Anything else?"

"I'm looking," Asher said. "They sent me several links." He quickly clicked the next one. "Oh, now that is a much better photo." It was the one he had sent them with the fishing boat. "They ran my photo through another program and cleaned it up. There's a name on the boat. I just can't pronounce it. Oh, good. They translated it."

Ryker came back around, and this time he just sat down and said, "*Wild Seas.*"

"Well, that's what we're looking for then," Asher said.

Another message came up. **It's registered to Awan Hania.**

He pronounced it slowly.

"Any connection to the brothers?" Ryker asked.

Asher asked Beau just that, who got back to him pretty damn fast.

Not on paper.
School friends?
Still checking. But possible.

Asher nodded and said, "No known connection to this boat is likely." He sat back and paused. "I'm considering, since one brother has already taken out two withdrawals from his bank account, it's quite possible that the mastermind behind all this gave them a cash amount too, so they could hang onto the girls until the ransom is paid."

"The real question here is, where are the brothers now?" Ryker said. "Because, as soon as we can put our hands on one of them, we can get more answers."

"If that brother is willing to talk," Mickie said.

Ryker looked at her and gave her a cold smile. "He'll be talking."

She winced. Just then Asher smiled and said, "Bingo. The van was caught on the traffic cams driving back toward the hospital." He quickly clicked on the feed, following its progress. "But it passed the hospital and has headed back toward that house."

"But it wasn't there when we were there," she said.

"Well, we picked up the woman, but her brother was likely the one punishing her."

"And, if they were in on it together, obviously there are some problems between the thieves," Ryker said.

Asher picked up his phone and made a call.

She wished there was something she could do. All she did was sit here and watch the two men work. Just then her own phone rang. She answered it to find Chandra at the other end.

"Any news?" her employer asked in an exhausted voice.

"Some," she said. "It looks like the twins have been moved to a fishing vessel farther up the coastline."

"Why would they do that?" she asked in utter defeat, as if this was all too much to comprehend.

"Because they're famous," Mickie said. "Their faces would be recognized no matter where they took them. They were taken to a hospital not soon after being kidnapped. Presumably Alisha was treated, and then both of them were released soon afterward."

"Well, has law enforcement been in to talk to the hospital?"

"No, not yet," Mickie said, frowning at Asher. "For that kind of stuff, you better talk to Asher."

"I will," she said. "I just wanted to get the insider news from you. So they still don't know if my daughters are alive, do they?"

"No. We're assuming they've been drugged to make them easier to deal with."

"Right. They never did like being told what to do."

"They like being separated even less," Mickie said. "So, chances are, they're together, and they'll stay that way. We must consider the fact that they might keep them drugged until this is over."

"And maybe that's better anyway," Chandra said. "The memories will be much less tormenting for them."

"Quite. Have you heard anything further on the ransom note? Any deadline for when or where to pay the money? Any insights at all?"

"No," Chandra said. "I keep hoping. But nothing."

"Were you serious about staying home more?"

"Yes. Remember that friend of mine, Deli, who lost her twins? She's heartbroken, and I realize how many years I have missed out with mine and that, if I wanted to have any future at all with them, I needed to scale things back again and plan on being at home more."

"Did the twins want you home more?"

"Yes, and, to be honest, I'm getting quite tired of this business. Even when dealing with people with this kind of money, people are still bridezillas all the way."

"You used to thrive on it," she said cautiously.

"I used to, but I'm getting older, and, after Deli's twins died, I just don't know. It's been like a paradigm shift for me to help me reevaluate what's important and what's not. It's like having that special lover from eons ago, who you broke up with for the silliest of reasons, and then, when it's long gone and over, and you can't get them back again, you realize what you've lost. It's where I am at the moment, like me making that reassessment right now before it's too late and spending time with the girls."

Mickie wasn't sure what to say about Chandra's analogy.

It hit a little too close to home for her. "What about your son? Does he spend any time with them?"

"No, he was always embarrassed by them," Chandra said, her voice quite sad. "He has never done anything to hurt them, but he never wanted anything to do with them either."

"That's because he didn't know how to treat them. They made him uncomfortable."

"They make everyone uncomfortable," Chandra said, once again exhausted. "I need to rest, but I want to touch base with Asher first." Mickie looked over to see Asher was off the phone. "Hang on," she said. She held out her phone to Asher. "Chandra wants to talk to you."

He took the phone from her hand without saying anything to Mickie. Then he turned to the phone. "Asher here."

She listened in as they talked briefly, and then he handed the phone back.

"Chandra, are you still there?"

"I'm here," she said. "He doesn't have a whole lot to tell me, and that's more depressing than ever."

"Stay positive," Mickie said. "We'll get through this."

"I know," she said, "but it's not how I want to live my life."

"No," Mickie said. "So, remember that. You have a chance to reevaluate who and what you want to be going forward."

"Right," she said.

Mickie hung up; sadness on her heart for what the older woman was going through. Mickie glanced over to see the men getting up. She looked at them and asked, "What's happening?"

Asher said, "We're leaving. Do you want to go back to

the hotel or be on a stakeout all day?"

Ryker headed to the counter and took care of their bill.

She groaned. "Can't say either appeals. Sleep would be nice. There is no other choice?"

"There's sleeping at the hotel," Asher said.

She shook her head. "No, I'll sleep in the back of the car."

"Then take a bathroom break here," he said, "because we're on the road again in five minutes."

BACK IN THE vehicle, Asher drove steadily, heading back to the house where they had picked up the woman. They had no idea if the other kidnappers had come back or not. The Mavericks team had assigned somebody local to watch the house, according to Asher's instructions, but Asher never heard back as to whether anybody had showed up here. He parked outside, turned to Ryker, and said, "I'll be back in a minute."

"Don't you want Ryker with you?" Mickie asked, leaning forward.

"No. I'll send a signal if I need backup."

"Good enough." Ryker shifted back in his seat and waved him off.

Asher walked up to the neighbor's side fence and followed it behind the house and slipped inside the same window he'd been in before. Then he stopped, listening for the sounds around him. Older houses made lots of creaking noises but weren't necessarily sounds of life. Asher and Ryker hadn't been told that anybody had returned to the house, but, according to the satellite, somebody had. That didn't mean that they had come inside though.

Would they have left the sister locked up? Or was that just a ruse? Asher wasn't sure. He quickly did a full scan on the lower level and then moved upstairs, only to confirm what he had been afraid of. The house itself was completely empty. As he sat here, he stared out the window, studying the layout and the neighbors.

A vehicle pulled up into the driveway. The lights shut off, and two men got out.

Immediately his phone buzzed. He pulled it out and said, "I see it."

He watched as the two men approached the front door. They weren't talking. They looked fed up. Asher slipped into the closet in the hallway and waited with the door slightly ajar so he could hear. The conversation was rapid-fire, and it was loud enough that he quickly recorded it, wondering if they spoke English at all. He ran the tape through a translator on his phone to get the gist of the conversation. They had needed money, and they need more money now. They had to get the twins back for the original supplier, but now they were in more trouble with the hospital who wanted money to pay for their services already rendered. They'd been forced to steal the women out of there and now had to pay a friend to keep them. They would ask their boss for more money because they weren't expecting the medical expenses.

Well, that meant the fifty thousand deposited in the one brother's account was all they got. No cash payment had been given to them after all.

As he listened and read the translation, he realized that one brother probably didn't know about the money in the account of the other brother. Asher couldn't tell which brother was saying they needed more money, but one was more adamant than the other. Chances were the one who didn't know about the bank account was more insistent because otherwise, although it would suck to tap into the money that they had counted as a profit for themselves, it was a necessary cost of doing this kind of business.

Just then they froze and called out, "Who's there?" The men went silent.

Asher quickly sent Ryker a message, only to have Ryker send back his reply.

I'm still outside. It's not me.

With that, everything changed. Asher quickly pocketed his phone, hoping like hell that Mickie had stayed in the car.

Only to hear a woman's voice snap, "You fools."

And he realized the sister had somehow been released and was back home again. He used the translation app on his phone to understand the conversation.

"Why?" one brother asked. "Why the hell are you not downstairs where you were supposed to be?"

"Because I was helped to escape," she said sarcastically. "Government assassins are after you now."

There was a shocked silence, and then both men yelled and screamed over each other's words to be heard.

And Asher realized that the sister he had rescued, who didn't know what her brothers were doing—maybe not in all the details, certainly knew enough.

"You must return the women now," she snapped.

"We can't," he said. "You know that we'll get in further trouble if we do that. We're supposed to keep them until we're told what to do."

"And yet, you already took them to a private hospital," she sneered. "And the assassins know about that. They know that you've got them on a boat up the coast."

"They can't know that," one cried out.

"But they do," she snapped. "They have satellite images. They followed you. They found you from the hotel, and they tracked your vehicle all the way."

"No," one said in a breathless voice.

"Yes," she spat. "And they'll be here any second. If they aren't already." She started to laugh. "Good God, did you guys screw up or what?"

"We didn't screw up at all," the other brother said, his tone much more measured and controlled. "Did you tell them?"

She caught her breath in her throat. "Tell them what?" She tried to lie.

"You did, didn't you? Even though you knew it was our way of getting out of here, you lied to us. You gave us up, didn't you?"

"No," she roared. "I didn't know anything. Remember?"

But there was a hard smack, followed by her cry of pain.

"Tell us the truth," that brother said. "Did you tell them?"

"No," she said, but her voice was cut off, and a strangled scream erupted and then went dead silent.

Asher winced. He didn't know if she'd been silenced permanently, but she'd said all she would say for a long time. And, with that, he made his move.

CHAPTER 9

MICKIE WAITED ALONE in the car on the back seat, under a blanket, so nobody would see that she was here. She hated to think that the men would be very long. But, at the same time, she'd asked to come when Asher had gone in alone, and she'd been shocked and surprised when Ryker had disappeared almost as quickly. Now her surprise had turned to worry. The last thing she wanted was to be left alone in the vehicle, but she also knew she wouldn't hold her own in a fight. And what she'd understood from Ryker was that both brothers had just returned home. She waited and waited until finally her phone rang. She answered it quietly. "Hello?"

"It's me. You can come inside the house."

She immediately sat up and looked around, seeing the light cresting in the horizon. "Is it safe?"

"As safe as it'll get," he said grimly. "Both brothers and the sister came home at the same time. The police must have released her, but the brothers killed her."

Mickie gasped in horror. "I'm coming in," she said. "Are you sure she's dead?" She crossed the road and swiftly raced up the front steps and pushed the door open. There, she was met by a macabre scene. She pocketed her phone, walked over, and bent to check the woman's neck for a pulse. "They broke her neck," she said in horror.

"Yes. They figured out that she had told us where the twins were."

"But she didn't really," she said. "She just told us they went up the coastline."

"But also gave up the hospital."

"True," she said. She turned to look at the two unconscious men. "These men could be the kidnappers, but I really don't know."

"But it's possibly them?" Ryker asked.

"Yes, the same build and roughly the same height. But the original guys came in with weapons."

"We haven't found any weapons here," they said. "Do you have any idea what the weapons were?"

She shook her head. "No, I really don't. I've thought about it since, but it all happened so fast, and I was knocked out so damn fast that I didn't really have much chance to determine if it was a handgun or a rifle or just a stick."

"Exactly," Ryker said. "It could have been anything."

She sagged onto the closest piece of furniture and said, "Now what?" Then she motioned at the two men, still unconscious on the floor. "We can't leave them here, can we?"

"No," he said. "We need to get some answers from them before turning them over to the authorities."

"How will you wake them up?" she asked with a broken laugh. "They look like they're out for the count."

"They are," Asher said. But then he pulled something from his pocket and broke it in his fingers. He held the vial under the nose of the one. He came to with a half roar, lunging up from the ground, only to come in contact with Asher's hard fist. He sat him in a chair, Ryker quickly tying him up. "Now," he said, "you can talk."

But the man stared up at him, bleary-eyed, with a fury that terrified her, even though he was secured. She understood a little bit of the language but not enough. Asher was running the conversation through a translator.

"You killed your sister," Asher said in a conversational tone. "See? I already know that you'll go to jail."

"She's a woman," he said. "She betrayed us. We won't get jail time."

Asher's eyebrows shot up. He looked over at Mickie, and she shrugged.

"I wouldn't doubt it," she said. "The law here is not exactly the same as American standards."

"That's too bad," he said to the man, "because your sister didn't betray you."

The brother's eyes widened, and Mickie could see a shadow in his gaze but didn't understand what it meant.

"Of course, it might have been your other brother who did it though," Asher taunted him.

Immediately his fury and rage spewed forth.

Asher waited until this brother calmed down and said, "So we know that you took the twins out onto a friend's boat. But we want to know where the twins are right now."

The man shrugged. "I don't know. He's supposed to take them up the coast for a while."

"And how will you get a hold of him?"

"We weren't. They would get a hold of us for the next step."

"In which case, they would have contacted you already," Ryker said.

At that, the brother just stared at him but stayed quiet.

"Fine," Ryker said. "We'll call the authorities and get rid of this bloody mess here. Two brothers will go down for their sister's murder, and we'll be on our way."

"No, we should empty his bank account first," Asher said. "It's obvious that he's been paid to kidnap these American women, so that'll be an international incident, and we'll make sure that the Swiss government knows all about it. Not to mention the American government."

"You don't know anything," the brother said in English.

"Oh, I'm glad you speak English," Asher said. "That makes life easier. So, where's the money from?"

The brother went silent.

Asher shrugged. "I don't give a shit. Jail is too good for him. Let's bring him back dead."

"No, we need to make an example out of him," Ryker said. "They can't go kidnapping citizens of the Western world and hold them for ransom or for whatever the hell they want."

"Well, a couple elements are at work here. Who actually paid them to do the kidnapping and who is it that they're supposed to be ransoming them for? Because I still have trouble with this whole wedding thing."

At the word *wedding*, the brother's expression switched to one of confusion.

"Oh, is your English not that good?" Ryker asked.

"My English is fine," he said. "What's this about a wedding?"

Mickie wanted to jump in and pound answers out of him now.

"Why are you holding the women?" Asher asked instead. "You tell us that much."

"I was paid to," he said.

"Of course," Asher said, as if that made perfect sense. Which according to him, it probably did. "But for what purpose?"

"They wanted them out of the way," he said.

"Permanently?"

"No, it was supposed to be for a few days to a week, depending on how much trouble there would be getting the ransom."

At that, Asher and Ryker exchanged looks.

"Do you know why they wanted them out of the way?"

"Pawns in a chess board, they said."

"Well, we get that. Are you releasing them when the ransom is paid?"

Again the brother shrugged.

"Will you hand them off to somebody else?"

At that, he shifted uncomfortably but stayed quiet.

"Were you to pick them up for somebody in particular?"

"Look. I don't know what you're talking about. I was offered a lot of money to pick them up at the hotel and to hold them for a week at most. That's all I know."

"And what will you do with them in a week?"

"I'm just holding them," he said. "When I get the word, I release them."

"Where will you release them?"

"I don't know," he said. "I haven't been told."

"Sounds like bullshit to me," Mickie said.

Asher looked over at her, smiled, and said, "I would think so."

The brother looked at her and then slowly realized who she was. "I should have killed you," he snapped.

"You should have, yes," she said. "Because I'm the twins' nurse. And if you've hurt them …"

"Doesn't matter if I have or not," he said. "You'll never see them again."

And that stopped her and Asher cold.

"What do you mean by that?" Asher asked.

But the brother wouldn't say another word. Asher grabbed Mickie's hand and said, "Come on. I want to walk outside for a few minutes."

"And why is that?" Still, she went with him willingly into the kitchen. Anything to get away from the death behind her. But when she heard a hard smack and a muffled groan, she froze, her breath caught in her chest.

But Asher wasn't having anything to do with it. He moved her outside. "We need answers," he said calmly. "That man is only holding out from giving them to us because he thinks that we won't push the line."

"What line?" she asked in a daze.

"That we won't hurt him," he said. "And he's wrong. We'll do whatever we need to in order to get the twins back."

After all, the whole purpose of this mission, job, op was all about getting the twins home. Nothing else really mattered. Certainly not the scum who had kidnapped them, not even about the mastermind of this mess. She nodded, looked up at him, and whispered, "I know. And it's okay. I understand. Do what you must do."

ASHER DIDN'T KNOW if it was Mickie's nursing training or her time spent with Doctors without Borders or if she had just come to a point in time in life where she understood, but he was glad that he and Ryker had her acceptance. It was much harder to fight off somebody who was supposed to be part of their team, and yet, disagreeing with their tactics. He waited until Ryker called out, and then Asher said, "Stay here at the kitchen. Don't come into the living room, okay?"

She crossed her arms over her chest but said, "Fine."

He quickly returned to where Ryker was.

"He said the pickup and delivery would be in different places," Ryker said as Asher joined him.

Asher looked down at the man, whose eye was puffy and swollen and who now had a missing front tooth. "Which is only to be expected," he said, "so I hope he had more to offer than that."

"The pickup was ordered by a woman, but it's to be delivered to a man."

"Which still doesn't help us much."

"The voice was Western-speaking."

"Well, that's a little bit useful. Does he know who it was?"

"No," Ryker said. "Said he never heard the voice again."

"How did they know to contact him?"

"He'd done a job for somebody else a while back."

"And who was that?"

"He's not talking. And, as it's out of the scope of what we really care about, I wouldn't suggest we move in that direction."

"I'm fine with that," Asher said, "but I need more information."

At that, the prisoner moaned and said, "I don't know where they were supposed to go afterward."

"Well, you must know something," Asher said in exasperation. "You don't just take a phone call, go pick up and transport two people in the dark, and turn around and keep them for a week for no reason."

"A lot of money," he said.

"Sure, but are they part of the sex trade? We've got another case involving human trafficking," he said. "Believe me. We're trying to track down a lot of women."

But his prisoner shook his head. "No, no, nothing like that."

"So, who is picking up the girls?"

"An old friend. He's coming in to save them."

At that, they froze. "Are you sure?"

He nodded.

"And why the hell would he do that?"

He shrugged.

"Does this have anything to do with a wedding?"

"No clue," he said. "I don't think so."

"The mother is a famous wedding planner."

"I don't think so," he repeated.

"Was the mother involved in this?"

The man stared at him in confusion, the question not really entering his brain.

Asher tried again. "I'm asking you if the twins' mother is involved in this."

"I don't think so."

"And who is the man who'll rescue them?"

"I don't know," he said.

"When and where is this rescue supposed to happen?"

"Within a few days maybe. Out on the water."

"Interesting," Asher said. "Right now even? While they're out there in your friend's fishing boat?"

He shrugged. "When we get word."

"And did you tell your friend holding the women on this fishing boat that this is happening?"

He slowly shook his head.

"Then this rescue will likely end up with him dead. Is

that the idea?"

"I don't know," he muttered. "It's possible."

"What happened to the other two men who were involved in this?"

"Hired guns. I needed them to get the women out of the hotel room."

"Did you kill the gunmen afterward?"

He sucked in his breath, shook his head, and said, "No."

"So who killed them?"

He was silent for a long moment.

"You must have some idea," Asher said.

"I might," he said, "but I'm really hoping not."

"Why is that?"

"Because the only people who would care are the ones setting this up," he said. "But I didn't tell him who I was hiring."

Asher laughed. "But they've been tracking you two brothers and the poor guy out on the boat," he said. "And they took out your two assistants, the pros who did the kidnapping. You took out your own sister, and now the only witnesses left are just the two of you. So, once the mastermind behind this all has the girls where they want them, you guys are redundant, and you'll go by the wayside, like the first two men hired."

"No, no, no," he said. "I'm the boss here."

"You're not the boss of anything, and apparently you're on the verge of getting yourself knocked off too because, once this job's over, there's no reason for them to keep you."

"I'm valuable," he said.

"You screwed up by involving other people. I'm sure they didn't like that."

"I had to," he said. "We all need backup."

"Absolutely. But they obviously didn't like your choices."

"Maybe," he said. "I don't know."

"So, your friend on the boat already has an *X* on his life too."

He winced. "I hope not."

"Because this is a good friend of yours, isn't it? Someone you like, that you'd hate to see dead?"

He nodded slowly.

"And he did this as a favor for you, didn't he?"

He nodded. "I can still save him."

"And what about the women?"

"I don't care about the women," he said tiredly. "I just want this shit over with."

"When you take on jobs like this," Ryker said, his voice hard, "it doesn't matter what the hell you want anymore. You're now somebody else's pawn. And with two down, actually three"—he cast his gaze at their dead sister—"that only leaves three more to go."

"Did you kill my brother?" asked the man.

"No, your brother is fine for the moment."

"Then kill him, will you? I don't want him to know."

"Know what?"

"Know what I've done," he said.

"You want me to kill your brother, so he ends up not finding out what you have done?"

Yes," he said. "It would be much easier."

"What is it he doesn't know about?"

"I told him this was a good job. And that we would be safe."

He looked down, studied the brother, and said, "Is something wrong with him?"

The brother shook his head. "No, no, no. But he's a little simple. And he has these rages. He got really angry when I took on this job."

"Smart boy," Ryker said. "So your brother will find out that his older brother, who he loves dearly, has put them up for a job that'll get them killed."

"Not if you kill him now," he said.

"We don't arbitrarily kill people," Asher said in exasperation. "Otherwise, we would have already killed you."

"You should have," he said, nodding. "You really should have. Because, when I get out of here, I'll come back after you."

Asher smiled at him and said, "Yeah, and how will you do that?"

But the prisoner smiled up at him and said, "You think you're so smart. Without my sister, you had nothing."

"Yeah, but now we got you."

At that, the brother's smile was wiped away.

And just then his brother stirred. "What's the matter?" he said, sitting up and holding his hand to his jaw. "Vitus? What's wrong?" And he stopped and stared at the strangers.

Asher could immediately see the rage taking over this brother. He was a big boy too, so Asher looked at Ryker and nodded. Without warning, Ryker turned with a right fist uppercut under the jaw and knocked him back out again. The younger brother fell down with a hard crash and went out again.

CHAPTER 10

T HIS WASN'T THE way Mickie would choose to travel, hunkered down in the back seat. She kept out of sight as an unmarked vehicle arrived and then led the two brothers away, while Asher watched as a body bag was removed from the house too. Then the strangers all left.

Asher and Ryker walked back to her and got in the car. She asked in a subdued voice from the back seat, "Do you guys just make phone calls and have the world jump at your fingers?"

"We're on a job," Asher said. His voice was patient and calm. "What do you want us to do? Call the Shanghai police?"

"No," she said. "Maybe. I don't know. Who you did call?"

"A group related to our US government," he said. "We'll take care of this."

"What'll happen to the brothers?"

"They'll be interrogated for more information, and, when they've given over whatever they've got, they'll be taken to the appropriate Shanghai law enforcement division to be charged with the murder of their sister."

"It probably won't stick, you know?" she said, her voice teary-eyed. She pinched the bridge of her nose. This had been a stressful and exhausting night. She took several slow calming breaths. "What are we doing now?"

"I need to take you back to the hotel so you can crash."

"And what about the two people behind the scenes? The one who paid for this and the one who's picking up the twins? Or are they the same, I wonder."

"Another reason why we need to be on hand," he said, "to make sure that whoever it is who's faking this rescue doesn't get away with it."

"It's not like the one brother gave you much information to help track down the twins, did he?"

"No, not necessarily. But we do have a better idea. We just need to get out in a boat and find the twins ourselves."

"That won't be so easy," she said, wondering if she'd be along for the ride too. Not that she looked forward to another stakeout, this time on the water, but neither did she want to sit in a hotel and wait and worry, while they were off doing their thing. As it was, anytime she thought she heard a noise, she jumped through her skin to avoid thinking it had anything to do with them.

"It's what we do," he said. "We'll start quite a ways up the coast. We already have a boat waiting for us."

"I'm coming with you," she said.

The two men exchanged looks. Asher shook his head. "It's better if you don't."

"It would have been better if I hadn't come to China at all," she said. "But it is what it is. I'm here."

"True," he said. "So, now what?"

"I don't know," she said. "I could go back to the hotel, but, if you find the twins on that ship, you know that they could be in terrible shape."

"And they could be 100 percent medicated," Ryker said. "That's what I would do."

"Sure, but," she said, her voice fatigued, "chances are you wouldn't have gotten caught, and this guy already has, so we know that he's not as good as you. Besides, unless they understand Alisha's diabetes, the sedatives or the insulin could kill the twins."

"Maybe. But, at the same time, an awful lot of other things can go wrong. We must look out for you too, making you a liability we can't afford as well."

"I don't want you looking out for me," she said. "I want you looking out for the twins."

"We won't save them to end up with you in trouble," Asher said, "so just get that out of your mind."

"I don't want to get that out," she cried out. "I just want this all over with."

"You're obviously exhausted," he said. "So, if you're coming with us, lay down flat. Pull up the blanket over your head, and go to sleep."

She stared at him for a long moment, wanting to kick and throw things, and yet, she knew it was precisely because she was so exhausted. She stretched out on the back seat as the vehicle drove off. She pulled the blanket up over her and said, "You didn't use to be so bossy."

"You didn't use to be so argumentative."

She gave a half snort at that. "Maybe, if I was, it would have been easier."

"What does that mean?" he asked, half turning to look down at her.

She smiled up at him. "I was kind of lost in your shadow back then."

"What are you talking about?"

"I was so insecure, and you were bigger-than-life, larger-than-life even back then. Your personality, your physique, everything you were, ... it was like the best of the best. Whereas I was the worst of the worst, and I wasn't heading anywhere."

He stared at her in shock.

She shrugged. "It's how I felt."

"And you really think that's how I saw you?"

"No," she said, "but I knew that would wear off when you realized life with me would be dull and boring."

"And how could it possibly have been dull or boring?" he asked. "I loved you."

"You did. But you didn't really know me. You didn't really see me."

"And because you thought I was in love with a mirage, you broke up with me?"

"I broke up with you so you could move on and have a better life," she said. "I joined Doctors without Borders so that I could at least feel like I had done *something* with my life. That was a great way to gain medical training, so I could continue to help others."

"And yet, at no point in time did you ever really deal with the fact that you should be helping yourself?" he questioned.

"My grandmother really helped me get things together," she said. "Mentally, emotionally."

"In what way?" he asked.

She shrugged. "She was really smart. And she kept getting me to deal with the fact that I am who I am, and who I am is just fine, and I didn't need to change for anybody."

"What kind of changes were you doing when you signed up for Doctors without Borders?"

"I was following your footsteps but trying to be different," she said as she yawned. "If you were such a fine example of humanity, I wanted to at least do something to improve. But Doctors without Borders turned out to be such an emergency-room situation, and that wasn't me. It wasn't who I was meant to be but somebody else. Instead, I should have gone into private nursing earlier. Because I'm really serving humanity then."

"Oh, I get it," he said in surprise. "So, you joined Doctors without Borders because you thought *that* was the right thing to do. You went into medicine because you thought *that* was the right thing to do too. What was it that was *truly* the right thing for you to do though?"

"To go home and look after my grandma," she said. "That was the right thing for me to do."

"For then." He studied her closely. "What's the right thing for you to do now?"

"Take the twins home, help them adjust to life again, and then do something else."

"Why something else?"

"Because I don't want to care for other people right now," she said. "I want to do a few things for myself."

"I'm glad to hear it," he said. "Just exactly what would that entail?"

"Well, you'll be busy traveling the world," she said, "so obviously I won't spend time with you." She heard his shocked gasp and realized what she'd said. She lifted a hand. "Forget that. I'm too tired to know what I'm saying."

"So, you don't mean it?"

"I don't even remember what I said," she said. Another yawn broke free. She tried to shake the fog from her brain. "Seriously I have no clue what I just said." Of course she did, but she wouldn't let that rear its ugly head.

"Good night," she said. And with that, her breathing fell

into a deep and heavy pattern.

⚓

"IS SHE REALLY asleep?" Ryker asked.

"She is now. I'm not sure what she was talking about either."

"What she was talking about," Ryker said, "makes a whole lot of sense to me."

"I don't think so," Asher said. "Not a whole lot of that was rational."

"I think what matters is, what do you want to do about this? What do you want out of the relationship?"

"I'm not sure. It never occurred to me that she wanted to spend time with me. That there was even another chance at a relationship to spend time in."

"No, because, in your mind, that relationship was over. But I think she's seeing something that she never really walked away from."

"That doesn't make any sense either," Asher said, twisting around for another look at Mickie.

"How heartbroken were you when she broke up?"

"Devastated," he said shortly. "She was my everything."

"It sounds like her own insecurity broke you up though and that she's finally figuring out who she is."

"Yeah, just ten years too late."

"But not too late if it isn't too late for you."

"Meaning?"

"It's never too late," Ryker said. "Think about it. There are all kinds of reasons to try a relationship again."

"No," he said. "The last thing I want to do is get dumped again because of her insecurities."

"I don't think she would now," Ryker said. "Sounds like she's come a long way."

"Maybe," Asher said, but he wasn't sure. But neither could he stop looking back at her and seeing that same young girl who he'd fallen in love with. "How could she think she wasn't good enough," he wondered out loud.

"Young girls," Ryker said. "They don't necessarily make sense. You just accept that that's her insecurity and help her grow past that."

"I didn't even know about it," he said. "How was I supposed to deal with it?"

"You didn't then," Ryker said, "but you can now. But that would mean going down that relationship lane again."

"I'm not sure I'm ready for that."

"Did you ever have another relationship since?"

"Sure," Asher said. "Several. Just none quite the same."

"Of course not. You didn't care for them because you still cared about this one."

"Just means I'm a fool," he said. "She was my one and only love. It never allowed me to feel that deeply again."

"No," Ryker said. "No emotion is foolish. Especially not when you love deeply already. You've always been like that."

"Maybe," Asher said. "But that doesn't mean I want to go in that direction again. That's just suicide."

"No, that's called *second chances*."

"Who said I wanted one?"

"Doesn't matter if you want it or not," Ryker said. "It's waiting there for you. But the thing is, are you too scared to step forward and take it?"

"Fear has nothing to do with it."

"Actually, in this case, fear has everything to do with it," Ryker said. "I already know you care. I see it in the way the two of you look at each other. I can feel the energy in the room when you two are together. So that's not the problem. Trust is. And more than that, there's fear. She walked away from you because she was afraid she wasn't enough. And you're not willing to take a step in her direction because you're afraid that she'll repeat her actions from back then."

"And that's where the lack of trust factor comes in," Asher said. "I gave her my heart, and she threw it back at me."

"Maybe," Ryker said with a head nod. "But she's in the process of handing you *her* heart. Will you give her the same treatment?"

"No," Asher said, "because I won't accept it in the first place."

"Too late," Ryker said with a gentle laugh. "Not only did you accept it ten years ago but you haven't actually given it back. She's in stasis, waiting for her life to move forward, and so are you because still you hold her heart in your hands."

"But I don't want to."

"It doesn't matter if you want to or not. The fact is, you've been in this position for the last ten years," he said. "You've never changed in the meantime. It means that a big part of you really wants it."

"Well, that part of me can just take a hike," Asher said. "If she wasn't the woman for me back then, she's not the woman for me now."

"She might not have been the young girl for you last time," Ryker corrected, "but that doesn't mean she isn't the perfect woman for you right now."

At that, there was nothing more Asher could say.

CHAPTER 11

N O WAY WOULD Mickie let Asher know that she was listening to any of their conversation, but she was damn glad she'd heard it. Mickie was exhausted and drifting in and out of sleep, but, when she caught parts of the conversation, she couldn't possibly go asleep again. She lay here, wondering if it was possible to have a relationship with Asher again. Did she even want that? She'd walked away last time, thinking she didn't deserve him. The ten years hadn't changed a lot, but it had changed enough of Mickie to become her own woman. She'd gone through enough that she'd built herself up inside to understand more about who she was and why she was where she was at. Her grandmother had been instrumental in getting her to this point. Mickie hadn't lied about that.

Her grandmother had been one of those unique people with a view of life that had just mesmerized Mickie. Sometimes her grandmother would say things that Mickie would stop and think about, and her grandmother had a most contemplative turn of phrase that made Mickie see the world completely differently. She missed her terribly. She figured that was why she had accepted the job to look after the twins. They had needed her as her grandmother had needed her. Was Mickie ready to let go of that?

At the same time, the twins really needed each other and

their mother more. They wanted more silence and solitude, to enjoy their gardens and their pets, and to interact less with the outside world. Which just brought Mickie's mind back around to Chandra. Why the hell would she have brought the twins to Asia? But then again, the twins had been modeling and had lived in this world a lot, but, for them, it was a compartmentalized time of their life that they had managed to shut down afterward.

It was just so confusing. Was it Chandra's out-of-the-blue and deliberate act to say, *Yes, you need one more experience, and then we'll keep you at home?* Why would she even push it on the twins? But lots of parents made decisions for their kids. Which, in this case, both of the twins were more susceptible to their mother's wishes. And it was much easier to get one on board and then the other one would follow.

Even now Mickie couldn't imagine how the twins were feeling. Such pain and torment coursed through Mickie that she desperately wanted a happy ending. Otherwise, it would haunt her for the rest of her life. When the twins were upset, their pain was so deep, and yet, so visible that everybody else around was affected by it as well. Of course it would be that much easier to keep them unconscious, so nobody around had to deal with their emotional outbursts.

But still, it wasn't fair. If the twins were awake, they would have left Mickie some written messages. She knew that. They loved puzzles; they loved games, and they used to draw Mickie Mouse all over the place. Not the words but that simple little four-fingered hand or just the big ears, like on a headband, the two symbols of Mickie Mouse. They were universally recognized. She sat up, slowly thinking about that and then grabbed a piece of paper from her purse and drew the very simple eyes, head, and ears and held it up to the front seat. "Did you ever see this drawing, even portions of it, inside the vehicle where the twins were carried or anywhere along the route where the twins have been?"

Startled, Asher turned to look at the piece of paper. He frowned as his finger gently traced the outline. "I'm not sure that I have. Why?"

"The twins would draw that," she said. "Anytime they were hiding, they would leave me a clue or a puzzle piece, if they were hiding."

"They would draw that when they were hiding?" Ryker asked. "Doesn't that defeat the purpose?"

"But it's only for me," she said. "That's a Mickie Mouse."

Enlightenment crossed both men's faces as they connected the famous Walt Disney character to Mickie's name.

"They must have loved your name," Asher said.

"They did," she said with a laugh. "They loved it, and they always thought that I had some magical connection to that world."

"Did they ever go to Disneyland?"

She laughed and nodded. "That's the one place we did go, and it's definitely sensation overload," she said with a smile. "But they loved it."

"And how did you figure out the connection?"

"Seeing the world through their eyes, it's like being shown a completely foreign universe," she said as she sagged into the back seat, staring down at the small design she'd put on paper. "They have such a unique way of looking at life."

"Do you think they would have left you messages?"

"If they could, if they were awake, and if they understood what had happened. Per the brothers' sister, the twins were screaming for me when with her brothers," she said

113

quietly. "Probably when they first woke up after being drugged to get them out of the hotel."

"But, since you and the twins were drugged from the initial kidnapping event, likely the brothers made sure the twins were drugged again, right from that moment on."

"Sure," she said. "But the twins are close to six foot and long and lean. You can't exactly pick them up and stuff them in a suitcase."

"Meaning that, somehow the twins would have been disguised to move them anywhere, correct?"

"Correct."

"Starting at the hotel-room kidnapping, those two gunmen probably sought out the easiest way—a laundry hamper," he said. "Down into the laundry room and out, awaiting pickup from the two brothers."

She thought about it and nodded. "That would make more sense than trying to carry them."

"Particularly with those famous faces," he said.

"Their photos are out there, so you'd recognize them," she added. "But some people are really recognizable in their photos, even if retouched. But those kind of photos are so much more than who the people are in them. In this case, the twins are so much *more* than their photographs. It's one of the reasons why they were so famous because everyone was trying to capture that elusive extraspecial element to who they were in a photograph."

"And do they have any special abilities, like memorizing dates and times from decades ago?"

"No, they're not Mensa geniuses." She chuckled. "They're just beautiful young women who wanted to be left alone."

"We'll find them," Asher said firmly. "We already know

roughly where they are."

"Yeah, so some idiot can come and rescue them," Ryker said in disgust.

"You realize this all sounds like stories made up, right?" She found this whole nightmare too fantastical to believe.

"True enough," Ryker said. "I was trying to figure that out myself."

"But why would anybody make up a scenario like this?" she asked.

"To hide exactly what's going on," Asher said. "But remember how it comes down to really basic motivations—power, money, sex, and greed."

"Unfortunately the sex part is a huge issue," she said, "because the twins are very beautiful women. But because they aren't quite the same as you and me, they don't understand the same sexual innuendos and flirting, like everybody else does."

"Meaning, they're likely still virgins?"

"I think so, but I'm not sure," she said.

"Huh," Asher said, as if considering that from a different perspective.

"Think about how people like to possess beautiful things," Ryker said. "They don't always want to touch them. They just want to keep them."

"Back to that pet scenario," she said with disgust.

"Let's not get ahead of ourselves," Asher said. "It could be anything, and yet, nothing."

"We should be there soon, shouldn't we?" Mickie asked.

"Soon," he said. "Another ten minutes or so."

"And what's the plan then?"

"Not sure," he said quietly.

"So either you don't have one," she said, flopping down

onto the back seat lengthwise, "or you don't want me to know about it."

"Our plans are fluid," he said cheerfully. "But don't worry. We have some."

She snorted at that. "As long as it means getting the twins back safe and healthy, then I'm fine with that."

"Got it," he said. Then he turned to look back at her. "When we get everybody back home to Switzerland, what are your plans? I understand you went home to care for your grandmother. I presume she's passed away if you moved to caring for the twins?"

"Yes, that's exactly what happened. As for plans–I'm not sure I have any," she said. "I now realize that I was staying with the twins because they needed me. I wasn't quite ready to let go of that. My grandmother and I were very close, and losing her was very debilitating. The twins filled a void that helped me to adapt to my loss, to deal with my own grief."

"And so, are you ready to move on?"

"I am thinking about it." She nodded. "I don't know how the twins will handle this though."

"That remains to be seen," Ryker said. "They probably need their mother more than anything."

"Maybe," Mickie said. "The problem is, there's just enough distance between them that I don't know if Chandra can cross that divide any longer."

"You must hold out hope for that," Asher said. "All families and all relationships can be mended, if people are willing to put in enough time."

As she lay here wondering, she had to consider if his words were meant on a different layer as well. Was he saying that their relationship could be mended? She didn't think so because they were very different people. It didn't mean that they didn't have the opportunity to have another relationship though, something different, something based on who they were today. Because she sure as hell didn't want to go back to that insecure young girl she had been before.

ASHER STUDIED HIS sideview mirror. "You see what I'm seeing?"

"Yes," Ryker said, checking out his rearview mirror as he shifted lanes. "I've been watching them weaving in the traffic. They've been on our tail for the last five minutes or so."

"Think it's on purpose?"

"Hard to say," Ryker said. "I would have thought we'd gotten away free and clear but ..."

"It's possible that we've been followed the whole time, and there have enough different people and cars to pass off to the next guy and the next guy and then next one. So we don't realize we've got a tag team of people following us. The question is who though?"

"Exactly. Do we have a double-cross happening?"

Asher looked at him. "Okay, that's something I hadn't considered. In what way?"

"What if the brothers were paid to take the twins, but then somebody saw an opportunity to either remove the twins from their care and demand more money or the brothers themselves decided they needed more money to look after them?"

"So, the original person who ordered their kidnapping hired somebody else to take them away?" Asher thought about it. "And the trouble is, once again, we don't have any answers." He looked down at his laptop. "We are getting steady satellite feeds in and along the coast and any number of boats that we're looking for."

"Ask if anyone is tracking the name of the boat yet."

Just then a message came through. "The chat box located Awan Hania, the boat owner's family."

"Should we start there?"

"No point," Asher said, his voice darkening. "Apparently a house fire took them out this morning."

"*Odd* coincidence," Ryker said, his voice low and soft, deadly.

"*Ugly* coincidence," Asher said. "I wonder if anybody knows yet."

"Meaning, the guy whose boat the twins are on?"

"Yeah, because, if he isn't dead already, he'll go into hiding as soon as he finds out. I doubt he'll see the fire as accidental."

"Depends if he lives on the edge of the law or if this is his first time doing something like this," Ryker said. "He's also likely to dump his cargo."

"We must stop that from happening. I suggest we head to the house fire first."

"Instead of the dock?"

"They're pretty close together," Asher said.

As that first stop was only a couple miles away, they made their way to the smoking ruins of the house. It had been put out by the local fire department, but it had damaged another house on one side. Other than that though, no further damage had been done to the surrounding neighborhood.

"The fire seems to be very isolated," Ryker said.

"Definitely arson," Asher said in a harsh voice. "If autop-

sies are done, I'm sure they'll find the bodies were dead first."
He turned and said, "I'll ask around. Can you stay with her?"

She popped her head up from the back seat. "I'm fine here," she said. "Just let me sleep."

He snorted, shook his head, and said, "No, that's one of the dangers of you coming with us. Somebody has to be with you at all times. Especially if we're being followed now." He ignored her glare and headed to a couple American-looking tourists, standing and watching. He identified himself using one of his fake IDs in law enforcement for Interpol and asked, "Do you know any of the details?"

Surprised, they shook their heads and said, "The fire woke us up early in the morning. We're staying here for a month but had gotten to know the family pretty well."

"Did the whole family perish?"

"Their son Ming took off four days ago, in the fishing boat. He'll be devastated when he hears."

"Four days?"

"He came back a couple nights ago, and he was pretty excited about a new deal," they said. "And then he left to meet a buddy, and we haven't seen him since."

"Did the family know about the new deal?"

The two men looked at the fire behind him. "If they did, they're not talking," they said.

Asher could see the strain on their faces, their pinched lips, and their bleak eyes. "I'm sorry. It's hard to lose friends, isn't it?"

"I was just talking to them last night," one said. "They didn't seem to think anything was different or untoward."

"Their son often take off on these new jobs?"

One man shook his head. "No, according to the parents, he's always looked after the family fishing business pretty steadily. They're not too happy about this new deal, but they didn't say much about it."

"Of course not," Asher said. "Tradition is so strong in most of these areas."

"With good reason," the younger man said. "In the West, we forget about things like that, and we end up always embracing the newest and the best technology. But it loses something as you move forward."

"China was built on families and traditions and rules," Asher said quietly. "Often new ideas or a new opportunities are met with disbelief and almost disgrace."

The men nodded, still staring at the burnt remains.

"Did the family say anything about where Ming was going?" Asher asked.

They shrugged. "The father mentioned a village up the far side."

Immediately Asher could feel something stir inside. Finally he had found a decent lead.

"And, of course, the father didn't give any details about what Ming was doing, did he?" he said in a light tone. He looked back at the family's home and said, "It might have eased the parents' minds to have known some details."

"Supposedly Ming said he couldn't tell them anything. It was a secret. I think that just made his parents feel all that much worse."

"Well, let's hope it's all legal and aboveboard," he said, studying the smoldering embers. "Because, if it wasn't, it could be what caused this house to burn to the ground."

The two males looked at him. "You think this was deliberate?"

"It's pretty intense for having been localized to mostly one house," Asher said quietly. "Definitely looks like arson to me."

Both of the men nodded slowly. "We wondered about that, but we didn't want to think it out loud. The law enforcement around here doesn't like anybody sticking their nose into their business. We've already been told to back off and to stay off."

Asher nodded. "I hear you. I'm looking for the son. I'm glad he wasn't caught up in that fire, but I'm sorry for the rest of his family."

"It was all of his family, as far as I know," the taller of the two men said. "I think his sister was in there too."

Asher winced. "And that leaves just the son to maintain the tradition."

Then they said, "We'll head back inside ourselves now. It's a depressing start to the day." And, with that, they gave him a smile and headed off. He studied their strong, young backs as they walked. Not military-bearing straight, more like college-age youthfulness, here for a new experience.

As he watched them hold hands, he considered that maybe this respite was a break from the stressful lives they lived at home, where here they could just be themselves and be together. Here, not too many people interfered in other people's business, especially with foreigners. As a matter of fact, foreigners could get away with all kinds of behaviors that other people couldn't. Still, Asher returned to the car and quickly shared with the other two what he'd learned.

"I gather we now we have a new destination," Ryker said.

Asher nodded.

"Well, let's head to the village then." Ryker quickly turned on the engine, and they pulled back out onto the main highway, while Asher looked up the location on a map.

From the back seat, Mickie asked, "Do you think his family was killed because of Ming's involvement?"

"I think that's exactly what happened," Ryker said.

Asher, without lifting his gaze, said, "And now people are following us again too."

"Good point," Ryker said.

Mickie's head popped forward. "You mean, we're being followed right now?" she demanded.

"A car was parked at the top of the road when we came past," Ryker said. "Two men sitting in it. Both with brush cuts. Both look like they had some military training. Both were Asian."

"So hired muscle but local," Asher said.

"Potentially, yes," Ryker said. "But we can't make any assumptions at this point."

"No," Asher said, "not about any of this. Because I don't think it's anywhere near as clear-cut as we thought it would be."

"No, it never is, is it?"

CHAPTER 12

MICKIE FOUND IT hard not to turn and stare behind them as they drove along the road. They were heading into much denser population and then coming back out of it into a much sparser population. She'd never seen so many people, and still tons of carts and people walked in the way of vehicles, as if they had the right-of-way. Hopefully the vehicles would stop for them.

And the vehicles she did see weren't as new or as expensive as anything in the Western world. It's not that China was poor but that the rich tended to stick to the more populated areas. As Ryker headed up the coastline, the landscape became definitely more about farming and fishing villages. And yet, the whole way, the vehicle following them stuck on their back end.

"What if it's Chinese police?" she asked.

"Could be," Ryker said. "But you'd think they'd identify themselves."

"Not if they're looking to see what we're up to," she said.

"Maybe," he said but didn't offer any other theories.

"Then what difference did it make?" She laid back down on the back seat of the car, her body so tired it couldn't sleep, and her mind so tired it wouldn't shut off. It just rolled endlessly on the same loops. She was enjoying nothing about this ride. But then it wasn't for enjoyment. It was all about finding the twins. When her phone rang, she jumped and pulled it out to check her Caller ID. "Hi, Chandra." Mickie put her phone on Speaker.

"Where are you?" Chandra demanded.

"Driving up the Chinese coast heading for a small village." She caught Asher's expression as she said that, and his headshake as he mouthed, *Don't tell her details.* Mickie balked at the moment, thinking about what he said and why not. Then she frowned at him, realizing he still likely thought Chandra was involved.

"Did you get a lead?" Chandra asked hopefully.

"One of many," Mickie temporized. "We're doing the best we can."

"And that may not be enough," Chandra said. "I got another ransom note today, delivered to my hotel. She wants me to bring a legally valid document, with my signature on it and my attorney's signature on it, transferring the twin's trust fund to her. She was very insistent that the transfer document was to be from me to the twins directly, and included any guardian in possession of them and taking care of them at the time. I'm to have it drawn up and executed in the next two days."

Asher nodded. "I saw that coming."

Ryker nodded. "Greed."

Asher shared a long look with Ryker. Asher whispered, "A change in the plan?"

"Or a change in the people?" Ryker added.

"And, if that was not enough," whined Chandra, "I also had some military police here today."

"Military police? Chinese military?"

"Well, they were Asian, and they identified themselves as

that, yes. I don't know if they were police. I'm not exactly sure what the term is here. But they were from the military, and they wanted to know what was happening."

"What did they want?" she asked, sitting up in the back seat and staring at Asher who turned to face her.

"I just told you that they wanted to know what was going on," she said testily.

"And what did you tell them?"

"I said that somebody had kidnapped my daughters."

She winced. "And did they offer to help you?"

"I think they more or less offered to throw me in jail first," she snapped. "They didn't like any inference on something that happened while we were in their country."

"No, of course not," she said. "Did they threaten you at all?"

"Of course not," Chandra said, sounding suddenly exhausted. "They said that they would send somebody over to help me."

"Of course. Did you happen to check their IDs?"

"Well, they had badges, but I don't remember who they were."

"It would be interesting to see if those IDs were real or fake," Mickie said, as she tried to think of all the possibilities going on.

At the sudden silence on the other end, Chandra asked, "Do you really think that's possible?"

"Yes," Asher said. "Tell her that it's quite possible."

Mickie glared at him. "It's just one possibility," she said. "I guess it depends whether anybody else shows up. Take pictures of their IDs and send it to us next time."

"*Us?*" Chandra asked. "Have you aligned with the two men I hired?"

"Somebody needs to be aligned with them," Mickie said quietly. "I'm here in case we find the twins, and they need me."

"What they need is their mother," Chandra said in a clear, crisp, and decisive voice. "If I ever needed anything to help me make that decision, this is it."

"Good," Mickie said, "so start clearing off your schedule and get to the point where you can stay home with them."

"Already in progress," she said. "I've offered to give clients their money back and/or to take on one of my two replacements."

"And, if you do that, what happens to a few of the people who work with you? Is anybody in danger of losing their jobs?"

"Wilson Chang potentially, but he can always move on to one of my two replacements. They've already been stepping up to do a lot more of the work."

"Sure," Mickie said. "But it doesn't have the same panache for him, does it?"

"No, of course not. However, if I step out of the game, he'll just work for my competitor or get out of this industry altogether."

"I guess what I'm trying to ask and not very well is," Mickie said, "what are the chances that he's involved in any of this?"

There was an ugly silence on the end of the phone. "God, I hope not. I can't imagine looking at everybody I work with and have lived with over the last several years to see if they're involved in some horrible plot like this to hurt my girls."

"People will be people," Mickie said quietly. "You need to think about it a little more. If you come up with any reason or any actions on anybody's part that's slightly sideways that could make them involved in this, you need to tell us and fast."

Chandra hung up as her only response.

Mickie sighed, put away her phone, looked at Asher, and shrugged. "Well, I don't know if it was the right thing to do or not, but I've at least got her thinking."

"Well, thinking is something she needs to do," Asher said. "There's nothing easy about any of this."

"But the fact is, somebody close to her knew that the twins would be here," Ryker said.

"But that could be all kinds of people, including strangers when the twins first came through the airport," Mickie said. "Their faces would have popped up. The media would have confirmed that the twins were here."

"And the media did post that too," Ryker said. "I caught all kinds of online articles on it."

"Well, that's great," Asher said. "That widens the pool of suspects."

"Not necessarily a bad thing," Mickie said. "Is it?"

"It's not a good thing either though," he said. "We have a ton of people to run down now. This could open up to any number of them." Just then his phone rang.

She laid back down and listened to the conversation. It seemed all that they did was send out lots of questions and get few answers back. As she sat up again, she realized the vehicle behind them was that much closer. "Ah, Ryker ..."

"I hear you," he said. "I can see them."

"Yeah, but do you realize that, if they ram us, we have no chance of surviving?"

"Oh, ye of little faith," Ryker said. As he raced up the highway, heading toward whatever destination he had in mind, suddenly the follow vehicle surged forward. As far as she could tell from the onboard GPS, Ryker's vehicle was heading in a straight line to a village. "We can't let them know about the village," she said urgently.

"I wasn't planning on it," he said.

As she turned to look back, the other vehicle had sped up so it sat right on their tail again. She tried to study the faces of the men, but they both had on sunglasses and wore hats. "I never realized just how much sunglasses and hats disguised facial features. It's ridiculous, but I can hardly even describe the men."

"You could try taking pictures though," Ryker said. "They won't turn out very good, but it's worth something."

Immediately she snatched up her phone and took as many photos as she could, aiming for as much clarity and focus as possible. "It won't help though," she said. "Those men are well hidden behind their disguises."

"And now that they know that we're aware of them," Asher said, "they'll take fewer chances."

"Great," she snapped. Just then the vehicle behind him sped up, almost to the point of banging into them. "Oh, I don't like where I'm sitting all of a sudden," she cried out.

But Ryker wasn't done outrunning them. Even as they spoke, her vehicle went faster and faster, and the other vehicle fell behind.

"They can't keep up," she crowed in delight.

"For the moment," Asher said. "Ryker can't do this speed all the time."

"So what are we supposed to do?"

"Get ahead far enough that we can ditch the vehicle and pick up something else," Asher said.

She stared at him in shock. "And where will you hide

this vehicle?"

Just then, moving at a speed that was scary fast, Ryker took several corners, sending her flying from one side to the other. When he hit the brakes really hard and then reversed, she couldn't even figure out where they were, until, all of a sudden, she was in complete darkness.

"Okay, what just happened?" she asked. "And are we safe here?"

"We are for the moment," Asher said. "But obviously we'll stand out like sore thumbs if we walk out in public."

"I know. We don't have any disguises to blend in here. And where are we?"

"We're at the village we were looking for," Ryker said. "And we have this space to hide in. I took advantage of this opportunity in case there were no more."

They quickly opened the car doors and stepped out. Asher looked back at her and said, "Come on, come on, come on."

She raced out her side and ran around to him.

He peeked through the gaps in the boards that made up the sides of this large shed. From the lingering smell, they were in a smokehouse.

"Is this where they've been hanging fish?"

"Yes, but that stock was taken a few days ago. Probably the older generation has died, and the younger generation isn't sure they're keeping it."

"So it's an empty building. Got it." As they stepped outside, she realized it was broad daylight. She had been underneath the blanket so much lately that she missed the first hour of sunlight, it seemed. She walked to a nearby clothesline. She grabbed an old scarf, wrapped it around her bright coppery hair, and tucked it under her chin. "It won't help much," she said. Both men found hats, and they wore them the same as every other person in this village—pulled down low. And somehow, as they walked, they seemed to shrink down in on themselves, making them look older, frailer, and definitely shorter. "I don't know how you two guys did that," she muttered.

"Practice," Ryker said cheerfully. "But the bottom line is, it doesn't matter because we can't keep it up for very long. It's meant to get us out of trouble but won't fool anyone long-term."

They quickly shifted to a pathway that led toward the water. As they meandered at a slow but steady pace, she picked up several walking sticks and handed them over. They weren't the finished sticks that they saw everybody else use in China, but they would do the job for right now. As a group, slightly one in front of the other, they made their way to the water's edge. There, tucked against the brush and the trees, a little bit back from the water's edge, they studied the boats parked here. A couple were farther out offshore too.

Just then Ryker pointed. She followed his direction to see a couple shipping vessels out farther and off to the side, in the area in between—loaded with fishing boats.

"But how do we know which one has the twins?" she asked.

"We check it out." His phone buzzed at that point in time. He grabbed it, read something on his screen, and said, "We must go up a little bit farther." And he led the way.

"To what?"

But he held up a finger. Frustrated, she fell in line behind him. If only she knew where they were going.

FOLLOWING THE GPS on his cell phone, Asher headed toward a small inlet around the corner from where they'd been initially standing. The path was rocky, a little bit rough, and populated with people, but no one was obvious or sticking out. It was just a small fishing village where people were somewhere along the water's edge and somewhere farther back. Everywhere he looked were boats though.

As he headed to the spot where his GPS told him to go, he could see one boat slightly different than the others. He immediately headed for it and found the keys in the ignition. It was a fishing boat but with an engine. That was much more his style.

With the three of them on board, he grabbed the long oar and pushed the boat out from the shoreline to deeper waters. There, for all intents and purposes, they looked like a normal fishing boat, except they had a powerful engine underneath. He turned on the engine, kept it in a slow gear, and headed out toward the other fishing boats. He didn't want to move too far and too fast. And it had to look more like he was out with everybody else. As he looked back, he saw Ryker throwing out some fishing lines. "If you catch anything," he said, "I get dibs on cooking your catch for dinner."

"Ha," Ryker said in a laughing tone. "I like mine just fried in butter."

"Well, I just like food," Mickie said. "We didn't bring any with us."

He chuckled. "No, but this boat comes equipped with everything we need."

She glanced at him in surprise and then opened the cupboards. And, sure enough, they could cook small amounts of food at a time, and they had some fresh fruit and some basic foodstuffs, including packs of cooked rice and cooked meat and vegetables. She immediately pulled out some of the food and said, "Well, I'll eat now then, because I have no idea what's coming." She made some wraps and offered one to Asher.

He looked at it, nodded, and took a bite. "Pretty good," he said. "Didn't know you could cook."

"I've gotten pretty good at being self-sufficient," she said, offering one to Ryker, then making one for herself.

Asher moved the vessel farther out into the open waters, heading toward the conclave of fishing boats ahead. He needed his binoculars, but, more than that, he needed to look a little bit more touristy than anything. He did a quick search around, studying the shoreline and the other boats that had come out behind him.

The three of them still wore their disguises. They were not much but it was enough that the fleeting eye would pass them before coming back for a second glance. And hopefully, by then, they were too far out. Then he turned to study the boats ahead of him. The most likely candidate was the one on the farthest side. He headed in that direction, giving the rest of the boats a wide berth, not knowing where their lines were and not wanting to get into an argument with any fisherman pulling lines behind them.

Just as he swooped outward toward the faster-moving waters, he heard Ryker behind him. He turned to see Ryker pulling in a big fish. Asher laughed. "So, we do get fresh fish for brunch."

"I told you so," Ryker said. He dispatched the fish with lethal precision and quickly had it gutted and fileted right in front of them. He deposited it in the ice box—filled with ice too—conveniently at the back of the boat, along with a small propane grill to cook the fish as well. If need be, they could stay out here for several days if they could fish. And while they had it, ... Ryker quickly lit the gas grill, laying the filets on the hot surface. "Sorry, Asher. Since you're driving, I'm cooking."

Asher just grinned and nodded.

"You've done that a time or two," Mickie said in amazement, when he served her one-third of the fish, freshly sautéed and smelling wonderful.

"More than a time or two," Ryker said. "We could use a few more of these though." He held the rod to her, as she scoffed the last bit of food into her mouth. "Go for it."

"I don't even know what I'm supposed to do," she said, holding the rod like it was some foreign tool.

"You'll never learn if you don't try," he said.

Asher laughed. "Fishing is a good sport, and it's good for the soul."

"Killing anything isn't good for anyone," she said.

He turned, looked at her, and challenged, "Are you a vegetarian?"

She shot him a look. "I'm not getting into that argument. I don't mind fishing, but I refuse to kill it."

"I can take care of that without any problem," Ryker said.

She snorted. "Nice," she said, but she willingly dropped the end into the water and let it run out on her reel. He quickly showed her how to stop it and then to move the rod back and forth slightly. "I feel like this is the wrong kind of fishing for here, like this is all set up for lakes."

"Deep-sea fishing has its own challenges," Ryker admitted. "But there's obviously a shoal of fish that's come in front of a predator, so don't argue. Just keep fishing."

She nodded, and Asher moved the boat gently, slowing it down so that her line would be a little more effective and so they'd look a little more like tourists on a trip than anything. As he saw his target, he cut the motor and let them just drift. He wanted to see who else was around. No sail flew atop the *Wild Seas* boat. It just sat here. "Ryker?"

"Yeah, it's anchored."

"Interesting. I wonder if anybody's aboard."

"I don't know," he said. "But it's the one we've been looking for."

"I think I'll head over and take a look."

"Good idea," Ryker said. "I'll stand watch."

Asher quickly stripped to his boxers and, on the far side of the boat, rolled gently into the deep water under the boat. Then he came up so that nobody would have seen him go in, and he swam toward the *Wild Seas*. It was bigger and probably twice the size of the one he currently had, but still, it didn't have the capacity to hold too much weight. The anchor itself was solid and would take a lot to dislodge it from the sea bed, which meant that they weren't too deep in the ocean out here. He floated around the side, looking to see for any way up easily.

On one side, he found a rope with knots. He quickly climbed up, slipped onto the deck, and down toward where the steering was. He found an open space to go below. He took one last glance around and headed down. At first, he could see nothing but darkness. Then shapes formed in the gray light.

On the side were bunks and a small kitchen and a little bit of a galleyway. Large holding tanks—which were fairly common on a fishing boat—plus lots of buckets full of fish heads, and a couple whole fish were here too. No fish still flopped, and the flies were pretty numerous. As a way to disguise the other aroma, it was pretty effective.

He checked everywhere inside that he could and found nothing. With his heart sinking, he knew the boat was deserted. He headed to the hold, quickly opened it up, immediately dropped into it and stepped back. Holding his nostrils firmly pinched for a moment, he quickly stopped the smell from overcoming him. The family line was no more. The fisherman, Ming Hania, son of Awan Hania, had been shot once in the head. Simple, effective. With another glance around the interior, Asher saw something that made him stop for a moment. A scarf. He picked it up and then slipped over the side and swam back to his boat.

As he pulled into their small fishing boat, Ryker and Mickie stared at him.

"And?" she asked, her voice on the verge of breaking up and leading to tears. "Did you find them?"

He held out the scarf and asked, "Do you recognize this?"

Her fingers closed around the material, and she nodded. "It's from Alisha's dress." She stared down at it with tears in her eyes. "Were they there?"

"No," he said. "They weren't."

"And what about the owner of the boat?" Ryker asked.

Asher shook his head. "He's there. But he's not alive anymore." He quickly explained what he'd seen. "So the twins have already been taken."

Ryker nodded. "Unfortunately that means we have no idea where they are or who may have taken them."

"But they couldn't have gotten far," Mickie said. "They haven't got that big a lead on us."

"No," Asher said. "But somebody knew they were here."

"Which means that somebody probably got the information from Ming's family," Ryker said.

"That's what I'm afraid of," Asher said. "And then they got here ahead of us."

"Well, those fishing boats were here when we arrived," she said. "What if they've got something to do with it?"

He turned to see two fishing boats meandering back toward the coastline. "We can't know until I can get some satellite imagery going," Asher said. "And I don't know if it'll be any good out here or not."

"Hopefully it will," she said, "but I wouldn't let those boats out of my sight anyway. It couldn't have been easy to move the twins anywhere, so another boat is by far the likeliest method."

"Particularly with Ming moored out here," Ryker said. "That's the only option."

"Or a floatplane," Asher asked.

"I think people would have heard it, and that would have caused much more of a nuisance than anything," Ryker said. "In this area, too memorable."

"I'm pretty darn sure we're talking about another boat." On that note, Asher, still wearing his boxers, slowly piloted the ship away from the one that held just the dead. "We need to tell the police," he said.

"I'll arrange that," Ryker said. "Our team can notify the police anonymously."

As Asher angled their boat toward the shoreline, he kept pace with the two boats ahead of him. He could see no markings to identify either of them. "Why two?" he asked Ryker.

"Disguise? Extra manpower? Maybe they're splitting up the girls?"

"They'll be sorry if they do that," Mickie said behind them. "If there's one thing in the world the twins cannot tolerate, it's to be separated."

Both men turned to look at her.

"I get that they're probably still drugged, but, as soon as they wake up, there'll be nothing but hell, and they will not be calm until they have each other, or until they are knocked out again."

"Right," Asher said. "But small boats are definitely easiest to work with out here."

"Easy to move one twin to one boat and the second into a second boat."

"And that explains why these two are sticking so close together."

"Well, we've at least got something to follow," Mickie said. "But it'll be pretty messed up if we get to the shore and these two fishing boats have nothing to do with the twins' disappearance."

"Absolutely," Asher said. "But we can track them. Track where they were, how long they were there, and if any odd movement between them can be seen. We can't forget that someone else was murdered. The police not only need to recover the body but also to find the killer."

"And is that happening right now?" she asked.

"Yes."

"It's so frustrating," she said. "The twins should have been given a tracker a long time ago. Like an ID chip."

"It's not all that common," Asher said. "In fact, it's still pretty rare for people to implant that chip."

"No, but I remember Chandra talking about it," she said. "I wonder what the decision was on that." She made a move for her phone and quickly called Chandra and put the call on Speakerphone. "Did you not get something like a tracker ID put into their wrists?"

"I did," Chandra said. "And they both hated it so much I had them removed."

"They could feel them?"

"They said it was a foreign body, and it was aliens or some such nonsense."

"Well, that sounds more like something somebody would have told them that," she said. "That's not something they would have dreamed up themselves."

"Maybe. It was likely Lana."

"Who's Lana?" Asher asked.

"Lana was the woman I replaced," Mickie said, her tone thoughtful. "Speaking of Lana, what's she doing these days?"

"I don't know," Chandra said. "And I don't care. The sooner that woman left, the better. I can't believe I was tricked into listening to her bloody stories all this time."

"I don't remember hearing too much about her."

"She was always making life very difficult for the twins. Things like, those trackers."

"Isn't she related to Wilson Chang?"

"Brother and sister," Chandra said. Her voice sharpened. "Why?"

"I was just wondering if maybe they had something to do with this."

"You keep harking back to it being somebody in my family or my business," Chandra said. "That gets very old, very quickly."

"I get that," Mickie said in a soothing tone. "But it doesn't change the fact that Lana left in an ugly manner. You fired her. And that tends to make for very upset people."

"I did fire her, yes, but I doubt she would have done

anything to have hurt the twins. She loved them."

As Mickie hung up, she looked at Asher and said, "Now I have a completely different theory for you to consider."

"And what's that?"

"Lana looked after the twins for a good ten, possibly more years. They traveled the world together, and they were very loving together. I know that the twins had been quite upset when Lana left. The twins didn't handle it well."

"Of course not. A big change for them," Ryker said. "Why did she get fired?"

"Because Chandra felt that Lana was inveigling herself too much into the twins' lives. However much of that opinion came from her son Edward. Chandra agreed but might not have seen it originally until he pointed that out. Then when she caught Lana talking to the lawyer about the twins, well, Chandra realized that she'd handed over too much control. She quickly nipped it all in the bud to make sure that nothing gave Lana access to any of the bank accounts, but it worried Chandra for a long time."

"And yet, she never mentioned Lana to us?" Asher couldn't believe it.

"You must understand that Chandra is big money. And servants and workers don't really have any involvement in her life. It's almost like we *don't have* lives."

He nodded slowly. "Interesting. So you're thinking that she didn't even consider Lana as a suspect, yet she was important enough to the twins to do something like this? And do you really think that Lana would kidnap the twins?"

"Her brother is Wilson Chang, Chandra's marketing manager. But more than that, they're half-Asian with ties to China."

Both men turned to look at her.

She shrugged. "I get it. I didn't figure it out myself either until just now."

"But would they hurt the twins?"

She gave them a wry smile. "You see? That's the thing. That's one of the reasons why it suddenly clicked in as to what might be going on. I don't think Lana would hurt the twins. I think she loved them."

"So what are you talking about?"

"I think that she probably misses them and decided that Chandra didn't deserve them. It's quite possible that Lana is doing this because she thinks the twins are better off with her than with anybody else."

CHAPTER 13

M ICKIE WAS KICKING herself for not even considering Lana before. "I'm sorry," she said. "Lana didn't get mentioned because of the way she left. It made Chandra livid to even hear Lana's name. And you never asked me if there were any disgruntled employees or anybody who would retaliate. You only asked about who would want to hurt the twins."

"Versus somebody who would want to take them away in an effort to save them," Ryker said, nodding. "And we're used to looking at everything from every angle, but that doesn't mean that we came up with all the right questions to make that information pop for you."

"It would make me feel a lot better if that's what's going on," she said.

"How so?" Asher asked.

"Because I don't think Lana would hurt the twins. She really cares. She was basically their mother for a long time."

"What's a long time again?"

She shrugged. "I'll say for over ten years, basically, I guess? The twins are thirty, and she was part of their modeling days, even their early adult years." She nodded to herself. "Yes, and I think she's the one who got her brother hired. But you can't quote me on that."

"I think somebody *is* telling stories," Ryker said.

At that, she gasped. "And that takes me right back to considering that maybe it's Lana." She groaned. "Lana apparently told lies really badly, and every time they got more and more elaborate. It's one of the reasons why Chandra finally fired Lana because Chandra could never find the truth of what Lana said."

"That bad?"

"That bad. For example, if some pocket money of one of the twins came up missing, Lana would say things like, *One of the other twins took it* at first. Then Chandra would be like, no, the girls have lots of their own money or whatever. So Lana would say something like, *Oh, well, a servant must have taken it*. Then it would be a break-in. Thereafter it would be something even stupider, like the twins would have mailed it to a fan or something like that."

The two men just stared at her.

She shrugged. "If you've never been around a notorious liar," she said, "you don't know how bad it is. Lana was a liar, which was very distressing to Chandra, but the twins loved the stories that Lana told them all the time—about how they were princesses and how this world was special for them."

"Lying isn't a good tactic when raising children," Ryker said. "Fairy tales are one thing, but then you must teach them about the reality of life."

"Especially with the twins. I think Lana also considered herself the reason the twins were so successful at modeling. Because she's the one who would coax them into doing what was needed. And ... she was why the twins stopped cooperating when Chandra forbid Lana from attending their sessions." Mickie had never really considered that point, but it made sense now.

"Right," Ryker said, nodding. "And, if Lana didn't get any extra money for her extra efforts, yet the twins were raking it in, then she might have felt that Chandra owed her."

"Chandra felt the twins owed her for their existence, since she gave birth to them," she said. "It was a very dependent relationship like that, and the twins missed her terribly, so I'm sure Chandra also felt that the twins needed her."

"Needed, wanted, depended on ... It doesn't really matter what kind of twisted relationship was going on. It obviously went on for way too long, whether the dysfunctional relationship between the mother and her daughters and then again the dysfunctional relationship with the daughters and their nanny. Do you know what Lana's ties to Chandra were?"

Mickie shook her head. "Chandra never said."

"So then, why hasn't Chandra told us about this?"

"I guess," Mickie said honestly, "because it ended badly."

"And Chandra obviously ignores the fact that Lana was her servant and was fired, so Lana's wiped off the earth because she's no longer in Chandra's orbit." Ryker nodded.

"Yes, but I'm not sure Chandra would agree that Lana had the brains for this either," Mickie added.

"She wouldn't need much in the way of a plan, would she? I mean, Chandra already delivered the twins to Asia. All Lana had to do was get help on this side," Asher suggested.

"And I'm afraid her plan may have changed," Ryker said, "because, even if Lana is involved in this, I highly doubt that she would be involved in all the multiple murders."

"No," Mickie said, "unless Lana's brother was involved,

and the two of them are fighting."

Asher stared at her in shock. "Are you serious?"

She shrugged. "Unless you've met Lana's brother, you wouldn't understand. But he's Chandra's aggressive marketing manager, and he's all about the bottom line."

"And Lana?" Ryker asked.

"I think she's more about the heart," Mickie said. "But I've never met the woman, so I really don't know."

As far as Mickie was concerned, this was a nightmare that kept going. She agreed with the guys. She didn't think Lana would have anything to do with drugging the twins or the deaths of the professional kidnappers and everybody else afterward. But, unless there was a falling out among thieves, the only other possibility was that Lana had lost control of the entire scenario. And that didn't bode well for the twins.

ASHER SORTED OUT what this new information meant in terms of the manipulation behind the twins' kidnapping. "In a way," he said, "it would be the best answer of all."

"Meaning," Ryker said, as they gently floated along behind the two boats in front of them, "you think that this Lana woman would be the one to keep the best care of the twins, in a kidnapping context."

"But only if she still has them," Mickie said. "If she has them, then she probably will look after them as if they are her own. One of Chandra's complaints was that the twins were looking to Lana more as their mother than to Chandra."

"Are the twins in any danger of making that mistake?"

"No, not at this age," Mickie said. "I don't think so. But

it doesn't change the fact that Chandra felt very much like she'd been usurped as their mother."

"And, if Chandra wasn't around very much, it would make sense, as the twins would become more dependent on Lana."

"Exactly."

"It doesn't change the fact that Lana could very easily have lost control over them now. Because, once we start talking about multiple murders here, the stakes have gone up."

"And that usually means hate or revenge," Ryker said.

"We can't rule out the other main motivators either," Asher said. He pointed to the two boats ahead of them. "Looks like they're setting out lines."

"A diversion?"

"It's possible," Asher said. "Go past them, and keep an eye on them."

With that in mind, the two of them sat opposite each other so as to see more without being obvious about it, while Asher piloted the boat slowly forward, his hat on, to all intents and purposes to look like locals moving across the waters. Nobody waved; nobody smiled, and nobody said a word. There was almost a tenseness to the atmosphere.

As they went past and headed around a bend, he said, "The two boats are following us now."

"Interesting," Ryker said. "I wonder where they're headed."

"Well, there's a place to dock up ahead," he said. "We could pull in there."

"Unless you are taking their spot," she said suddenly.

"Well, it's big enough for two."

"Making it all the more likely that it's their parking

spots."

"If it's a rendezvous spot, it would make sense because a lot of docks and decking are around. But they must carry the twins on land. That'll be hard to miss."

"Unless they're capable of walking right now," she said.

"If they've been drugged up until now, I would imagine they'll stay that way."

"Possibly," she muttered. Then she paused before bursting out, "I hate this. I hate this subterfuge. I hate the fact that we can't just board the boats and grab the girls."

"And what if the girls aren't there?" he asked.

"I know," she said. "That's why I hate it. I don't like games."

"All of life is a game," Asher said. "It's just a game you must learn to play."

"Maybe, but I can't say I'm terribly impressed."

"I hear you," Asher said as he headed toward the far side of a dock with just enough room for him to pull their boat in. There, he set them up against the wharf. "Now keep an eye out," he said. The two boats, sure enough, followed slowly and moved gently through the water, keeping close to the shoreline. They pulled up to those two empty spots as expected. "Bingo on that one," Ryker said.

"I know," Asher said.

Both men driving the two other boats hopped out and headed up the dock, neither seeming to care about what was inside their vessels.

"Shit," she said. "Were we wrong then?"

"I don't know," he said. "We must wait and see."

Just then a group of locals came down and started to harangue Asher.

"I guess we're in the wrong spot," he said. He held up

his hands in apology and gently pulled back and headed upriver again.

"Wow," Ryker said. "Very territorial, aren't they?"

"Most of this industry is," she said. "But you should probably stay in the trees, near where we had been earlier."

"I know," he said, "but it's a little harder to move here. I'll use the engine again." He bent down, turned on the engine, and slowly putted his way out past the dock where the two boats were. Ryker and Mickie kept their gazes on all activity on land, while Asher kept his eyes on the ocean ahead. This close to the shore, he knew it was way too easy to get his engine in trouble, which is why they had been using poles to move closer in. He moved out a little bit farther and then came back around, working with the currents and coming close up against the trees. Then Ryker threw a rope up around and caught onto a branch, at least keeping them in one place. From under the cover of the trees, they watched the two boats.

"How long are we waiting here?" Mickie asked after thirty minutes.

"As long as we need to," Ryker said.

"Unless I go take a look," Asher said.

"We're wasting time," Mickie said.

He could hear the fatigue in her voice and her frustration, turning to look at her. "You could have stayed at the hotel."

She glared at him mutinously.

He smiled, winked at her, and said, "Don't forget that, while we're here, we have other people working the satellites to see if the girls were taken anyplace. Nobody has contacted me with information yet. So this is still our best bet."

At that, Mickie subsided and nodded. "I keep forgetting you're not alone."

"And neither are you," Ryker said. "Remember that too."

She groaned softly. "Okay. I'm sorry."

"It's all right," he said. "But a lot of our work is sitting and waiting. We can't have anybody jumping the gun and giving us away."

"You'd think they'd have seen us already," she said.

"No, I don't think so," he said. "There's no real reason for them to have noticed us."

"Maybe. But, at the same time, it would be nice to finally get some answers."

Just then Asher caught sight of something that had him turning around. "Looks like we got some action."

Ryker joined him at the side, both of them peering through the brush. "He went to get help?"

"Both of them did."

"Look at that," he said, as they watched four extra men come down to the docks. There was an animated discussion going on. Two men disappeared into the first boat and came out carrying something all bundled up.

"And, from the looks of that, it could be anything from a dead animal to one of the twins to something just large and bulky," Ryker said. But then two men disappeared into the other boat and quickly brought out a matching package.

"Bingo," Asher whispered. "That's the twins."

As they watched, another large group of people joined them, and they all disappeared into the crowd.

Asher immediately hopped off the boat and said, "Keep an eye on it." He ignored Ryker's call to wait because Ryker knew that Asher had to go, and he had to go now. And no way could Ryker join Asher. Somebody had to keep an eye on Mickie.

CHAPTER 14

"**S**HIT," MICKIE SAID. "You need to go after him. He can't take on that many men on his own."

"No, and he knows it," Ryker said. "That's a large group. He's trying to see where the twins end up."

"You mean, if they go to a vehicle or to a house?"

"Yes," he said. He brought up his laptop and showed her. "I'm getting a satellite feed right now."

As she watched, he connected to one satellite, and the feed slowly came closer and closer and closer, until she could see herself distantly in a boat. "Oh, my God," she said. "That's really freaky. Talk about worrying that Big Brother is watching you all the time."

"It seems like almost anybody in the world can see what you're doing at any point in time if you're out in the open."

"And that's not something I want to ponder," she snapped. She pointed at the large crowd moving. "There."

"I know," he said. "It's almost like they're a diversion."

"It's hard to say," she said. She didn't understand. "What are they all doing?" As it was, she watched the screen, struggling to see. "Vehicles are all around there."

"Exactly," he said. "They're trying to hide what they're doing."

"And the crowd just became bigger and bigger and bigger."

"Dammit," he swore.

"Any sign of Asher?"

Ryker shook his head. "No, he's completely buried in that crowd. He's trying to see where the hell the twins disappeared to in there. They'll be passed off to someone, whether into a vehicle or into a house."

"This is just ridiculous," she said. She stared ahead and then watched as several vehicles broke off in different directions. "And how are we supposed to track all them?"

He quickly zoomed in and took shots of license plates. "That's how," he said. And, for the next ten minutes, he was incredibly busy as vehicle after vehicle after vehicle broke apart and headed away. Others came in from the highway above, while more came and moved and backed around, just generally confusing the issue.

"What kind of money would it take to get so many people to do that?"

"It depends," he said. "If it's all family, you only tell them that they're in danger and need help to secret these women away before they are harmed. Nobody'll ask any questions, and they'll all pull in to help. Particularly if they know somebody."

"Right," she said. "And the other option is they were paid."

He gave a bark of laughter. "Or there's that. In this downtrodden economy, everybody would do something like this for a few bucks. It's not like they're hurting anything."

"No," she said. "Everybody can use a few spare dollars."

"Exactly. The question now really is, what's the answer?"

"It's a scary thought," she said. "Can't say I think very much of any of this. It's all just puzzles and games." Then she cried out, "Wait." She pointed to the top of one feed where a woman stood. "Get closer to that."

Ryker quickly zoomed it in. "That's as close as I can get."

"What is that twenty feet above her?"

He laughed. "Probably half a mile of sky."

She stared at him in shock and then said, "Can you at least freeze it so I could look at it?"

He quickly took a screenshot of it and asked, "Who do you think it is?"

"I think it's her," she said. "I think it's Lana."

"Would she be here on-site?"

"I don't know," she said. "Maybe she would if she were supervising the removal of the twins."

As she watched Lana, another man came up behind her. He'd been standing a little ways off, but now he stood right beside her. The woman's body stiffened. Without even looking at him, she turned and walked away.

"What was that about?" Mickie asked, puzzled.

"Lana's following orders," Ryker said. His tone was dark. "This might have started out as her gig, but somebody else has taken it over."

Just then Asher came back through the trees. "Come on. I've got us a set of wheels."

"Did you see where the twins went?" Mickie asked. As she was helped off the boat, she stumbled and fell into branches that scraped at her skin and brushes that stung her face. She was then suddenly picked up and tossed over Asher's shoulder as he trampled his way through the underbrush, carrying her up to where it was much easier to walk without getting hit every three seconds. When he set her down to her feet, she smiled up at him.

"Thanks," she said. "I didn't realize how treacherous the

going was." She looked down at all the scratches on her arms. Several were bleeding.

"See if you can stop that," he said. "We don't want to leave a blood trail."

Immediately she nodded and used her T-shirt to press hard against the wounds. "It's minor," she announced. And before she even had a chance to register what kind of a vehicle he had, she was sitting in the back seat all over again. "Do you have any idea where the twins are going?" she asked.

"Yes," he said, "but we must catch up fast before I lose the vehicle." He hit the village roads and then up to the main thoroughfare. He turned left, heading back, and then kept on going.

"Oh, my God," she said. "Back the way we came?"

"Yes," he said, his voice hard. "It looks like it."

"And what do you think the crowd was?"

"A diversion," he said. "And it grew into more than just the initial crowd. Everybody else from the village came. A rumor went around that people were giving away free money, and everybody just piled in."

"That'll do it," Ryker said.

"It looks like Lana was there too," Mickie said. "Did you see her?"

"I possibly saw her, but I don't have a photo for her. Do you?" he asked, turning his head and looking at Ryker.

"Yes," Ryker said. "I'll get you one real fast." He quickly dug one up, and she could see Asher taking a quick look at Ryker's laptop screen.

Asher nodded. "Yes, she was there, but a big guy was behind her. I actually wondered who that guy was before I ever saw her."

"Super big?" she asked slowly.

"Depends what you mean by *super*, but, yeah, about six foot eight. Why?"

She took a slow, deep breath. "Because Chandra's son, Edward, runs several businesses, and his head of security is a similar height. Big white bald male. His name is Sweng, I believe."

Silence filled the car.

"Well, that could have been him," he said. "But we can't make any assumptions. Get an image on him for me. I got a good look at his face."

Asher picked up his speed and raced down the freeway.

ASHER HAD SEEN them load both of the women, wrapped up like mummies in blankets, into the back of a black crossover vehicle. And it had taken off among all the other decoy vehicles. Asher had watched long enough to make sure it headed back toward town.

Now he had to pick up the pace and get there fast, but he was a good ten to fifteen minutes behind. He checked his speed and then ramped it up higher. He passed several vehicles, then tucked into his lane again when he saw oncoming traffic and just kept on driving. "See if you can also bring up satellite feed to see where that vehicle is." He reeled off the license plate number. Then he watched as Ryker quickly opened up new windows on his laptop and sent requests.

"Use the chat box," Asher said. "It's faster. They've got more men on the other side."

Ryker quickly did as instructed.

Asher's mind raced. "What are the chances that Chandra's son found out what Lana was doing and decided to get in on the action?"

"I can possibly see that happening," Mickie said. "I can't imagine Edward starting this from the beginning, but, if he caught wind of it, it's hard to say."

"Especially not in light of a five-million-dollar ransom," Asher added. "But with the second ransom note now to include the twins' trust fund transfer—which is almost twice the money Edward needs to cover his eighty-million-dollar debt—I can totally see that happening."

Mickie nodded. "Plus, I've dealt with Edward before. It was unpleasant. But otherwise, I don't really know him and have never met Lana. I only know the bits the twins and Chandra have told me." Mickie paused.

Asher noted her hesitation. "Tell me what's on your mind, what has you thinking before you speak it out loud."

"Chandra once said Edward's out for himself. He sees things for what it can do for him." Mickie paused again. "She liked that because she understood it. He had worked for her for years but prefers to work for himself, developing commercial properties now." She shook her head. "I don't think he cared enough about her brand—or even her," she said. "But he must have come up with an angle that would work, and then I can see that being something he'd cash in on."

"Interesting," Asher said. "Does he know Lana very well?"

"After ten years of her being employed by the family, living at the estate with his mother and his sisters? Absolutely he does."

"Interesting," Ryker said. "Here's a visual on Chandra's

son, and he's got several of his business heads around."

"I'll take a look in a minute," Asher said. He watched the traffic, and, as soon as he had a break, he quickly raced past the next two vehicles, then tucked back into line and then did it again and again. "I must find a—no—take that vehicle," he snapped, "before we hit the town center and before I lose him. If they're more than five minutes ahead, I'd be surprised."

"Even five minutes is five minutes," Mickie said.

"I know," he said. "Just hold tight, sweetheart. It could get a little rough." The endearment had rolled off his tongue, and he had barely even noticed. From her reaction, he didn't think she did either. He didn't know what the hell was going on, but having her in his life again almost felt like she was sliding right back into the same place where she'd left from.

That couldn't be good because that meant Ryker was correct. That meant Asher hadn't moved on. That he'd unconsciously left that place open for her to return to. But, at the same time, it wasn't there for her. At least he hadn't expected it to be there for her.

He was too damn confused about it to spend more time contemplating it. This wasn't the time nor was it the place. They had to get these two women back before they were sent into the kidnapper's ultimate scenario. But what nightmare scenario could that possibly be?

His mind kept working through it as he wove through traffic, which was getting denser and denser. Finally he could see the vehicle up ahead. He needed one more break to catch up and to get at least two vehicles behind. As soon as a break in traffic happened, he whipped fast and pulled into a lane just before the sound of screeching brakes.

"Jesus," she said from the back seat. "Where'd you learn

to drive like that? Go-Karts?"

"If you mean, *That was damn fine driving. Thank you very much, Asher*, then I'll agree," he said smoothly. "If you're trying to tell me off for being reckless, I remind you that we have two women thrown into the back of that vehicle up there. And, from what I saw, they were either comatose or possibly dead."

When Mickie sucked in her breath, he realized just what a shock his words were. And, of course, he'd intended it to be a shock, but he didn't mean to upset her. "Look. I'm sure they are alive," he said. "Otherwise, there'd be no need for all the subterfuge. They could have deep-sixed the women in the ocean."

"Thanks for that," she said.

He shook his head. "I didn't mean it that way."

"Of course not," she said. "You just live in the moment and never think about the future, don't you?"

He always thought about the future. It was part of his mind-set. It was needed in each and every op he went on. He knew a minefield lay behind her question, so he was determined not to go there. He wasn't even sure where that statement came from. He didn't know what was happening, but, just because she was so emotional, he knew it would be difficult to get her back on track. "Why don't you just rest," he said in a soothing voice.

"*Rest*," she yelled.

He winced and groaned. "Fine. Sit back there, and be quiet then." At that, she shut up, but he could see from the rearview mirror that she was steaming mad at him. He shrugged. "I get that you're mad at me. You are always mad at me. That's just one of the facts of life."

"What do you mean, I'm always mad at you?" she

wailed. "Is that what you thought?"

"Sure. You used to give me that look," he said with emphasis, "then you'd turn away."

"That look was because I didn't understand what you were up to, and I was trying to figure out how I fit into your plans," she snapped. "Which is also why I figured I never could fit into your plans because I wasn't good enough."

"Good Lord," he muttered. "Sorry, Ryker. You apparently are getting another dose of our personal history."

Ryker laughed. "It doesn't matter. However, I must admit, something else did occur to me regarding the twins."

"And what's that?" he asked.

"Well, we've been talking about all these made-up stories of Lana's," he said. "Does this whole setup potentially have the makings of it coming true?"

Asher shook his head at him. "What are you talking about?"

"I get it," Mickie said from the back seat. She leaned forward and stared up at Ryker. "I wonder if that's what's happening?"

"It'd be the best-case scenario for the twins," he said.

"Maybe," she said, "but it still puts them through unnecessary trauma. For what?"

"The *for what* part, I don't understand," Ryker admitted. "When you think about it, considering where we're heading—and, of course, it's too early to know that yet—I wouldn't be at all surprised."

"Okay, I get it," Asher said. "You guys know something I don't know. But what the hell are you talking about?" Just then the vehicles in front all hit their brakes, and his hands were full trying to stop the vehicle from smashing into the rear bumper of the next one. He swore as the traffic slowly resumed again. "What the hell was that?"

"That," Ryker said, tapping his laptop screen, "was your black car disappearing from the main road."

Just as Asher almost passed the turn on the left, he saw the vehicle way up ahead on a perpendicular road. Asher quickly pulled their vehicle into the next lane, crossed the other lane, and disappeared down the side road, following the black vehicle. "That was fast on his part. I almost missed it."

"I know," Ryker said. "So it makes me feel like either they changed their plans at the last minute or knew they were being followed."

"My vote goes with being followed," Asher said. "Or they're even warier now."

"Most likely both," Mickie muttered.

He looked at her in the rearview mirror and then back at Ryker. "Now what were you saying?"

"I'm not sure what I'm saying," Ryker said. "But, if you think about it, the first ransom note was all about a wedding planner being forced to work with bridezilla, pointing the finger at the bride-to-be. Then Mickie updated us on the twins' history—which Chandra conveniently failed to tell us about—how that man in Spain had the twins taken years ago. But he was cleared. Our next theory was that it might be somebody who wanted to rescue the twins, not to hurt the twins. Which linked Lana to the current kidnappings. And, of course, now we've got firsthand knowledge that the ex-nanny is involved, seeing her on the scene just an hour ago."

"The storyteller, yes," Asher said. "So?"

"And what if Lana's the one who orchestrated all this?"

"But that's what we were thinking earlier," he said impatiently.

"Yes, but what if it's her son who's doing the rescuing?"

"Chandra's son?"

"Yes, what if the nanny started it, and the son realized that he could end up making this work to his advantage? He'd jump in, save the twins from Lana, and now he's got his men pulling the twins back to the hotel to be the savior."

"And yet, do you think it was set up like that from the beginning?"

"I doubt it," Mickie said. "Edward's too selfish to care about the twins."

"So then why would he have any interest in rescuing them now?" Asher asked. "At least the second ransom note would transfer the twins' trust fund to him. What does he get if he doesn't cash in on the ransom demands?"

Ryker turned to look at Mickie behind him. "What do you think?"

"He'd get his family's undying gratitude," she said quietly. "And, because the twins have been unconscious hopefully through most of this, Edward can make up all the stories he wants and can still have control of their lovely trust fund."

"It doesn't make any sense to me," Asher muttered.

"It doesn't because you're not thinking about being a brother who was always out in the cold because the twins took everything the mother had for attention and love, then money too for the twins' ongoing medical needs," she said. "Because now the mother will be undyingly grateful, and the sisters will be undyingly grateful, and, as the man in the family, with a retiring mother and difficult sisters, everybody'll turn everything over to him. Then Wilson Chang is out of a job for sure. Remember? A lot of money is involved, and someone needs to manage it."

"So you think Edward manipulated this from the beginning?"

"No, I still don't think Edward was part of the original plan," she said. "But he must have jumped on board thereafter. I don't know. We must talk to him."

"Yeah, he was involved," Ryker said. "About the time that second ransom note came through would be my guess."

"I agree." Asher nodded. "And, Mickie, you think this Sweng, the head of Edward's security, is the one bringing the girls back to the hotel?"

"I wouldn't be at all surprised," Mickie said.

"Call Chandra," he urged. "See if she has talked to her son recently."

"Why?" she asked, pulling out her phone.

"Because maybe she's already got word that the twins are on their way back," Asher suggested. "Something she has failed to tell us about as well. Or … maybe she got word on the ransom drop. Because, after all, somebody needs to get paid out of this. So, if we're wrong about Edward's participation in all this, then maybe that's how the ex-nanny gets paid off."

"God, the webs we weave," Mickie muttered behind him.

"Hey, it's all about opportunity and being opportunistic," he said. "When something like this happens, all kinds of people jump on board to get a piece of the pie. Because, right now, Chandra is willing to pay almost anything to get her girls back."

"So her son gets to ride to glory," Mickie added, "and won't get the cash ransom money but will end up with a bigger paycheck over the long-term."

"Absolutely," Ryker said. "But, in the meantime, somebody'll get blamed for all those deaths. Who's that? Who's behind all of those?"

"I don't know," she said. "That's still left to be determined."

"My vote is with the brother," Asher announced.

"No," she said. "I doubt it. But I wouldn't be at all surprised if it wasn't her brother."

"Yes, that's what I said," he said, "the brother."

"Which brother?" she asked. "Too many are involved."

"Not the twins' brother. Not the dead sister's older brother. The *nanny's* brother. Because what does he get out of this deal? He gets nothing if she hands them over Edward."

"And that won't sit well with Wilson."

CHAPTER 15

MICKIE SLOWLY DIALED Chandra, wondering how she was supposed to formulate the questions even now surging through her brain. Could there be so many people so close to Chandra who were just absolute assholes? When she heard Chandra answering the other end, Mickie frowned and held back saying anything. A note of excitement in her employer's voice was something Mickie didn't recognize.

"Hello?" Chandra said. "Is that you, Mickie?"

"Yes," she said. "What happened?" She glanced at the two men, Asher driving and Ryker desperately keeping track of the vehicle in front of them now that they were well into the town city limits. The traffic was crazy.

Asher glanced in the rearview mirror to see her face, trying to figure out what was going on.

Mickie hit the Speaker button and said, "You sound really excited. Has there been news?"

"Yes, yes, yes," Chandra said. "But it's not for sure yet. But I can't stop being hopeful."

"What happened?" she asked.

"My son's got a line on what's going on."

"Seriously? Edward?" she asked. "I didn't realize he was looking."

"Of course he is," Chandra said in a warm, glowing tone. A tone Mickie had yet to hear from Chandra. Only to have Chandra's tone turn caustic. "They are his sisters too, you know."

"Of course," Mickie said quickly. "I didn't mean anything by that. I didn't realize that he was in the loop and actively doing something about it. Of course he knows though."

"Ever since they went missing, he's hired private investigators," Chandra said. "But we didn't realize because he never told me."

"Of course. Edward is used to running his businesses on his own," Mickie said with a nod. She rolled her eyes at Asher, who was listening. "Well, I'm really glad to hear he's found some good news."

"With any luck, we'll have answers, and potentially the twins will be back within an hour or two," she said; she sounded like she was almost out of breath.

"Are you okay?" Mickie said instantly. "You sound short on breath."

"That's because I'm dancing around the room," she said, laughing. "This is the best news ever."

"But is it just a line on information or have the twins actually been rescued?" She studied the traffic ahead and could see the black cross over vehicle in front of them.

"Well, Edward didn't want to tell me too much information, just in case," she said. "And I respect that. But I also know my son. And, if he can do something about this, he'll do it, and he seems to think that he'll get them back here anytime now."

"Wonderful," Mickie said warmly. "In that case, now I don't really have anything to report ..."

"Come back. Come back," Chandra said. "They'll need you."

"Well, it sounds like they've had quite an exciting adventure," Mickie said. "At least I hope that we can make it sound like that."

"Well, that'll be the story that they'll get told, and we'll stick with it," Chandra said. "We know perfectly well that they'll take on whatever we present to them. They'll have their own fears to deal with, and I'll hire the best psychologist that I can. But not here. Not until we get back home to Switzerland."

"Of course," Mickie said. "But you don't know when you're heading home, do you?"

"Well, I'm so confident in my son," she said, "I have flights booked back tonight."

"Commercial flights?"

"Commercial? Gosh, no," she said. "A private jet of course."

"Oh, of course," she said slowly. "And did you book me one too?"

There was a startled surprise, and then Chandra said, "Oh my, I completely forgot."

"Oh," Mickie said, feeling very disoriented with the sudden turn of events. "Is there room on the private jet for me?"

"I'm not sure," Chandra said. "But don't worry. I'll make arrangements for you to get home too." And then she said, "Oh, I must go," and she hung up.

Mickie stared at her phone in dismay. "Well, you heard all that," she said. "Which makes me feel like potentially Edward *is* involved in this somehow."

"Well, from what she said, yes," he said. "That's very suspicious."

"I know," she said. "But I'm a little perturbed that they

didn't think about me flying back either. As if I'm not even part of the equation."

"Right," Asher said. He quickly changed lanes again. "What's your relationship been like with them?"

"Friendly but businesslike. I'm an employee. Obviously I'm not family," she said but couldn't still the bewilderment inside. "But it's like she didn't even consider me."

"Well then, she just got some of the best news ever apparently," Asher said. "So you must go a little easy on her over that."

"Right. Of course," she said, but it was hard to still that sense of disquiet. "She's making plans to rush back to Switzerland."

"Which is what we would all do in her situation," Ryker said reassuringly. "Just think about it. This is the place where they've been kidnapped, so she wants to go home where she feels like the twins will be safe and secure."

"Right," Mickie said quietly. She stared out the window, trying to shake off that odd sense of dismissal from that conversation.

"Are you worried about going back with her?"

"No, she'll get me home somehow," she said. "If nothing else, a commercial flight."

"But you don't feel like you count all of a sudden, right?"

She gave him a smile. "It's funny because, when you're interacting with the whole family, you feel like you're family too, but, when you're not there, you realize that you really aren't part of the family. You're just an employee."

"Exactly, yet surely she won't leave you here," he said. "But, if she needs you for the twins, it's odd that she didn't even consider that you would need space on that private jet.

And what private jet? Does she own one?"

Mickie looked at him in surprise. "No, she doesn't. But she has multiple friends who have them. So it could be any one of them. She has an old friend. A long-term male friend," she said with emphasis. "He has a small Learjet that they fly all over the place in."

"Any idea how many it holds?"

She slowly shook her head. "No. I've never been invited on board. It wasn't the one we flew in on."

"Well, I wouldn't worry about it," Ryker said. "There'll be the four of them for sure, plus any security guards or head of security that might be with them."

"A daunting thought," she said, sagging back. "How long until we're back at the hotel?"

"At the rate we're going, about ten minutes," Ryker said. "If they slow down or try to shake their tail, it could take us two or three times as long."

"Do you think they know that we're following them?" she asked.

"I would think so, yes," he said, "especially from the way they're moving."

She nodded. "Okay. That makes sense."

And just then Asher swore. She straightened and tried to look through the traffic, but it was streaming all around them. She asked, "Did you lose them?"

"They crossed several lanes of traffic and booked it onto an off-ramp." Asher pounded the steering wheel as he maneuvered his way past and through. By the time he got off the massive freeway, the crossover vehicle was several miles back, somewhere caught up in the suburbs.

"Well, that was a deliberate move on his attempt," Asher said. "So obviously they knew they're being followed."

"And what's our best tactic at the moment?" Mickie asked. "Wait for them to return to the hotel where the twins will be delivered?"

"That is quite likely our best avenue, yes," Asher said. "It'll be interesting to see who brings them in."

"But what we don't have," she said, "is any way to know if they'll be transferred from one vehicle to another."

"I know," Ryker said. "And I could lose all of today just trying to backtrack and find them here. Better we head toward the hotel, which isn't very far away now, and see if we can capture them or find them as they head in."

"And do you really think that we'll have a confrontation when we do?"

"I highly suspect," he said, "we'll find the brother is there as the savior, and the twins will be carried up to the hotel, and a doctor would be called immediately to check on their condition, while everybody celebrates."

"And that's seriously scary," she said slowly. "Because the brother has a lot to lose if he's involved in this and we can prove it."

"He has a ton to lose," Ryker said. "So we can't trust anybody who's involved."

"Including Chandra?"

"The thing is, right now, she's all about getting her daughters back. She won't want anything to do with finding out who did this. All she's interested in now is getting the twins home safe."

"Don't you think she'll want somebody punished?"

"Well, not a lot of damage has been done in a way, has it? Her reputation is intact, and she's quickly shedding clients and distancing herself from the industry, so she can retire earlier and go home and spend time with the twins who she has ignored for so much of their lives," Asher said in a dry tone. "The brother, Edward, is now back in favor with the family again, although Lana needs to change her name and probably never show her face anywhere close to where Chandra is."

"Would the twins say anything about Lana's presence there?" Ryker asked.

"Well, it depends," Mickie said. "For one, were they conscious? For two, did they see her? And three, sometimes when the twins talk, nobody believes them anyway. It can be hard when they have a tantrum or go on a tirade. Most of the time, the twins keep repeating what they've seen over and over again until it's acknowledged. That could be the case now."

"Would the mother do anything about it is the question," Asher said.

"Smile indulgently, pat their hands, and tell them that she'll look after them from now on," Mickie said calmly. And suddenly Mickie realized that her job was coming to an end. It didn't matter if she was ready for it or not. With the mother going home and staying with the twins now as much as she could, that wouldn't really require Mickie's presence. And the brother, knowing that she might have some inkling of what was going on—particularly if she let him know in any way, shape, or form—would do his utmost to get rid of her.

As a matter of fact, he'd likely do that anyway just because she was connected to the mess here. She wouldn't be surprised if she was offered a nice little sum of money to leave quietly, all with the good intentions to keep the twins safe and stable.

"What are you thinking about?" Asher said.

"I think I'll need a new job," she said as she quickly out-lined her thinking.

He pondered that for a moment and then said, "That would make sense on Edward's part. He'll pay off everybody involved and make it all go away. But that doesn't stop the dead bodies from showing up."

"But all the dead are over here," she said. "As much as I hate to say it, what I don't want is for him to turn any of that suspicion on me." She saw the confirmation of her fears in his eyes.

"That would be a little too nice for him, wouldn't it?" Asher said. "He wouldn't even have to pay you that nice little payout."

"Particularly," she said, "when I wasn't even given a flight home."

ASHER HATED HER logic but had to admit there was just a little bit of something to it. So far, they've been running around in circles, and he needed to ensure that the blame wasn't conveniently dumped on Mickie's head. Since she was a foreigner, lost and alone, as soon as the police were contacted, and she was labeled as a suspect, she'd be taken in custody and thrown into jail. And the police wouldn't be in any hurry to clear her as a suspect.

Asher glanced at Ryker to see the taut line of his jaw. They exchanged hard looks.

With a nod, Ryker bent down and pulled out his phone and started sending messages.

That was the last thing Asher needed to happen here. Their own presence was in the same delicate situation. "We'll need a place to get out of here," Asher said.

"I know. I was thinking of that," Ryker said. "And we also have an awful lot of dead bodies to let everybody know about."

"I've been keeping a tally going," Asher said, "and letting our team know, but this will get a little bit ugly."

"What about the brother?" Ryker asked. "Will we try to deal with him?"

"You know what? I thoroughly suspect that we won't even get a chance to talk to him," Asher said.

Just then the traffic came to a complete stop with an accident up ahead, blocking off travel in the other section. Swearing, Ryker checked the satellite feed to see what was going on and said, "I see a couple big traffic accidents. I don't know how to get out of here again."

Asher squeezed past another vehicle and turned around and headed back the way that they'd come. That meant a big detour and more time lost.

"We won't get back in ten minutes now," Ryker said, reprogramming the GPS. "I bet we'll be at least thirty or forty minutes."

"Which means they'll get in ahead of us, won't they?" she asked.

"Yes," Ryker said. "They will, indeed."

"We can have men waiting at the hotel, but I suspect that, all of a sudden, the twins will appear, and Edward will be the one riding to victory," Asher said. "We need to be on damage control."

"Damage control?" She looked at him hesitantly. "What does that mean?"

"Your worst fears," he said. "We'll do everything we can, but there's been a complete shift right now. We need to regroup." He looked at Ryker and said, "And, if we can, we need to get in quietly."

"Do we still have our hotel rooms?" she asked.

"Yes," he said. "Ours for sure. I don't know about the one that you had with the twins."

"No, probably not," she said. "Oh, man, this just went to hell real fast." She yawned and reached up and ran her fingers through her hair. He realized just how tired and worn out she was and also how nervous and worried she looked.

"The good news is that the twins should be okay."

She beamed a bright smile. "And that *is* the bottom line," she said firmly. "If we've got them back, and they're healthy and fine, all the rest of it's extra."

"Maybe," he said. "What we can't do though is end up in trouble over this." He instructed Ryker on what to do.

With his phone open, Ryker quickly sent as many messages as he could with as much of the information as needed. His last line was **We need new rooms at the hotel.**

When Ryker got an answer back a few minutes later, Asher said, "We're not returning the same hotel. We'll take one over."

"That's a better idea," Ryker said. "And now the traffic's moving on this side too."

Fifteen minutes later, Asher pulled up to the new hotel. Ryker went in as the other two quickly grabbed up their bags and went through the back door, where he led them to a room on the second floor. It had a balcony facing the hotel where they were at.

"Shouldn't I go over there?" she asked nervously. "Not to mention to retrieve my bag."

"We'll come with you. Make sure you have your purse."

She had her big bag with her with all her traveling documents and her medical kit. "If I get a chance to go in that jet tonight, I should go, shouldn't I?"

"Not unless we are going with you. Let me confirm that," he said, checking his watch. "It's almost an hour since you talked to her. Let's go."

They walked down the stairs of the hotel across the street and walked into the reception area of their first hotel. Asher led her to the elevator, and nobody stopped them. Nobody seemed to care. He checked and said, "We should still have the rooms here too."

"So why aren't we using them?" she asked. Then she looked around. "Where's Ryker?"

"Taking care of business," he said calmly. When she continued to stare at him, he added, "He's checking out Chandra's most recent hotel room." They headed first to the men's floor, where he checked to make sure the rooms were still as Asher and Ryker had left them, which was ready for the next occupants, as the guys had all their stuff with them. Then he nodded, and they headed back to the elevator and went up two more flights. There they stepped out onto the penthouse floor, but there was already a hollowness to it.

Mickie studied the hallway and shook her head as she raced to the room where Chandra had originally been staying and knocked on the door. While Chandra had booked another room in a nearby hotel, she had maintained this one, in case needed once the girls returned. She had told Mickie that the three of them might spend the first night together as a family, to calm the girls down. She had also instructed Mickie that some of Chandra's personal toiletry items and a few of her clothes had been left here, so that Chandra could switch between hotel rooms without too much inconvenience.

When there was no answer, Asher moved her slightly back and using his tools, opened the door, stepped inside. Not only was nobody here but he saw no bags, no luggage, no personal belongings. Mickie spun around, stared at Asher in shock. "Did they leave? Without me? Already? How?"

"Well, they're gone from here," he said with a nod. "And Ryker just confirmed her room at the other hotel has been cleared out." He waited for Mickie to react. "Remember that she didn't necessarily have you booked on that private jet anyway."

She stared at him in shock.

He opened his arms, and she ran into them. He held her close while he tried to figure out what was going on. "Let me check to see if they left anything," he said. He quickly did a search, his instincts saying that they bolted rather than were kidnapped.

"Did you find anything?" she asked anxiously. She stood in place, her arms wrapped around her, and her fingernail in her mouth as she chewed on the tip.

"Not yet," he said. "I want to make sure they left voluntarily and haven't been kidnapped."

As her jaw dropped, he nodded. "We can't take any chances at this point."

Then she raced around to help him. He quickly sent a message to Ryker to tell him the hotel room was empty.

"What about the room that the twins and I had here?"

"Let's go check," he said with one last glance at the huge suite. They stepped out into the hallway and made their way down to the room that she had shared with the twins. She still had her key, so she quickly unlocked it and stepped inside. "Well, they're not here," she announced.

"And neither is their luggage," he said. He walked over

174

and found Mickie's luggage instead.

She cried out, "Look." He turned and saw an envelope on her pillow. She walked over, picked it up, and said, "It's got my name on it."

"So open it up," he said. "Let's see what it is."

She found a note from Chandra. He sat here and waited while she read it, and she looked up at him with shock on her face. "She said that she trusted the information on finding the twins. They were meeting somebody who was bringing the twins back, and she was taking them out of the country immediately. She's sorry she didn't have room for me on the private plane too, and she would send information on a new flight for me to get home."

"But she hasn't actually sent you that flight info, has she?" he asked.

She checked in the envelope and shook her head. "Nothing else is here." She pulled out her phone and quickly sent a message to Chandra, asking where they were.

"She can't answer you if they're already in the air. And," he added, "chances are she won't answer you anyway right now because her focus is on getting the twins out."

She swallowed, nodded, and said, "Still sucks."

"Yes," he said. "But it's not the end of the world. We can deal with this."

She nodded. "I hear you, but I'm a little unsure that she'll send me that ticket."

"What did you text her?"

"Just asking where she was," she said. "But I'm now asking for a flight home as soon as possible too."

"Well, hopefully she does that for you," he said. "Does she have a secretary or somebody to arrange that for you?"

She nodded and quickly switched to a new contact. "I'm

doing that right now too." Then she looked around the room and said, "I don't even know if I'm allowed to stay here anymore."

"I suggest we go downstairs and find out the details," he said firmly. "An awful lot of rooms are here that potentially are empty and are not paid for—or are empty and paid for— that we can use if need be." He tossed a final glance around the empty room. "Okay. Let's go find out, and we'll come back and get your luggage if need be."

Downstairs at the reception desk, he asked for Chandra and was told that she had already checked out.

Then he gave the clerk the room number that Mickie was in and asked how long it was paid for. The clerk checked it out and said, "It's been canceled. The cleaning crew is supposed to go in there later this afternoon, as it's been booked already for this evening."

Beside him, she swallowed hard.

"I see," he said. "Well, we'll grab her luggage then. Sorry for any inconvenience. And what about these rooms?" He quickly asked about the other two rooms assigned to him and Ryker.

The clerk looked those up and said, "Those have been canceled and turned over as well."

"Meaning, new people are coming in sometime this afternoon?"

"Exactly," he said.

"Fine. Here are the keys for those rooms. We'll get her luggage, and then we'll hand over the keys to her room."

With that, they dashed upstairs and grabbed her luggage, then came back down and returned the key. Asher led her out of the hotel and over to his newly booked rooms.

"Did that just happen?"

"Yes," he said. "And it makes me leerier of the fact that

you may or may not have a flight home."

He could feel her tense up. It was one thing to be deserted in another country. It was completely different to be deserted in a foreign country where you didn't speak the language and when a trail of bodies had been left behind. If you were one of the visible faces on the case was an entirely different scenario too.

Back in his new hotel room, he dropped her luggage on the side and said, "Now I need you to sit quietly while I make some contacts and phone calls."

She looked up at him and nodded. "Are you planning on leaving without me too?" The cry from her heart broke his. He walked over and wrapped his arms around her and held her close.

"I couldn't do that to you," he said. "I couldn't have done it to you ten years ago, and I couldn't do it to you now."

She whispered, "I'm so sorry."

"For what?"

"For walking away last time," she said. "I knew immediately it was the wrong thing to do."

"And yet, you didn't come back and tell me that," he said with a note of humor in his voice.

"No, because I firmly believed that you were better off without me."

He tilted her chin and kissed her hard. "So maybe you should rethink that now."

She stared up at him. "Really?"

He nodded. "I guess I haven't found anybody else to love in all these years, so maybe, just maybe you're the only one for me."

And he kissed her again. This time she wrapped her arms around him, held him close, and kissed him right back.

CHAPTER 16

A<small>ND WHAT A</small> *kiss it was*, Mickie thought.

Still crappy timing as Asher gently nudged Mickie toward the bed, but she went willingly.

"Why don't you sleep a bit? Things will look better when you wake up."

She could only hope for that. They'd crossed a divide and were at someplace new.

Someplace new.

She had never expected to get here. But since then, she couldn't resist it as an option. She had never lost track of him and had never lost sight of him in her heart. He'd always had a place there, and she'd struggled hard to find somebody else, but it never happened. Asher was a very special man, and she'd been a fool. And she couldn't believe how she was so lucky to have him right now.

At the same time, she was devastated that Chandra had left Mickie behind, not even paying for her hotel room. She had money of her own, but she wouldn't have ready access to it right now. Sure, her credit cards could be used, but this wasn't part of her job description. It wasn't the deal. And she hadn't had a chance to make sure that the twins were okay either. That was devastating. She loved those two women. Sure, they were not the easiest people to handle, and she hadn't worked with them for all that long, but they were very special. Their hearts and souls were pure delight, and Mickie would miss them.

But, after this stunt, no way would Mickie work with Chandra again. And Mickie was afraid that it would get much worse before it got any better, particularly if Edward was involved. She'd been around him a couple times, but he'd been notoriously unnoticeable. He was just a man, yet another one busy in business who didn't give a damn about anything but himself. And that was real life.

Still, she was stuck now and was not sure where she was supposed to go or what she was supposed to do or who would even have a return flight booked for her. She sure hoped that Chandra arranged one for her, but what if Edward said that he had already, and she'd left him to handle it all? And what if Edward didn't plan on getting Mickie home at all? What if he planned on making sure she never made it back anywhere?

Being left as the culprit for all these murders in China was one thing, but what if Edward had something much uglier planned? What if he planned to make sure that she just was another body in the long trail? No answers, no questions, no leads, and everything would go cold. She'd be yet another statistic in a country full of foreigners' deaths.

Depressed and upset, she sagged onto the bed and closed her eyes. All she could wish for was that maybe, just maybe, Asher would lie down and hold her close until it would all be okay. Because she knew in her heart of hearts that maybe they'd get there, but, right now, there was absolutely nothing okay at all.

ASHER WATCHED AS she crashed on the bed. This last couple hours had been shock upon shock upon shock, and he could well understand her feeling completely abandoned. What he didn't know was whether Chandra was behind it, or if her son Edward was behind it, or if they were both in this together, or whether they were just so focused on getting the twins out of the country that they had forgotten about Mickie—or had they completely planned this from start to finish? Because of all the people who had arrived in this country with Chandra, the only one not leaving was Mickie, which deserved an awful lot of explanation, and yet, Asher didn't have the answers.

As a matter of fact, with a little bit of work on Chandra's and Edward's parts, they could leave enough evidence behind to make it look like Mickie was the culprit all along. While Asher waited for answers, he had already made plans to get them out of the country on the sly themselves. He needed to head back to the US base in South Korea as soon as Ryker checked in. And that would take a little bit of doing too. Just then his phone buzzed. It was Ryker.

We need to leave now.

Swearing, he hopped up, walked over, gently rolled Mickie onto her back, and gave her a hard kiss. As her eyes opened, he said, "We must go, and we must go now." She stared at him in shock and then bolted upright. "Use the washroom and maybe get a drink of water, then we're out of here." He grabbed their bags and condensed them down into something he could easily carry on his back. As soon as she came out of the washroom, he grabbed her hand, and they disappeared out into the hallway.

Even though they had paid for their room here, unlike where Chandra had supposedly paid for their rooms in the first hotel, Asher knew that either the local police or the Chinese military or another paid entourage that he didn't want to meet were coming to this hotel. It wouldn't take the armed men long to get past the front desk either.

Once in the hallway, he headed out the back exit, worrying that he would even now be too late. He raced down the stairs, his heart pounding, knowing that she was doing her best to keep up with him, and he wasn't giving her any opportunity to slow down. He hung on to her hand firmly. When he hit the second floor, he stepped onto what was a small deck and dragged her with him on the steps, straight down and out into the back garden. He didn't change direction. He didn't even look around. He kept on going, keeping her firmly at his side. When they were finally around a corner, she asked him, "Are we safe?"

"Not safe enough," he said, his tone curt, urging her forward still. "I don't know who or what that was about, but I got word that we needed to get out, and so we're out."

"Police?"

At her quavering voice, he realized she was on the edge of losing control. He pulled her a bit closer, wrapped an arm around her shoulder, and just hugged her tight but kept her feet moving forward. "It'll be fine," he said.

"How can you say that?" she cried out.

"Because I've been here before," he said. "I've never yet not made it home."

At that, she looked at him, nodded, and put a little more juice into her footsteps, so he didn't feel like he was dragging her down the sidewalk. "Where are we going?"

"We've got to get out of here," he said. "The fastest way to do that is to cross the water."

"To the base again?"

"If we're lucky," he said. They were still several blocks away from the water, and he kept up his zigzag motions as he tried to find his way to get them across.

"Ferry?"

"No," he said, "likely private."

"That'll leave a trail," she warned.

His phone buzzed. He dropped his arm from around her shoulder and pulled out his phone and saw it was Ryker. He swiped his phone. "Hey, we're about two blocks away from the fish market. Where are you?"

"I'm at the market. As soon as you come down the center set of docks, veer right and go past three different moorings. I'm down on the seventh, on that last mooring."

"On the way," he said. He pocketed his phone and grabbed her hand. "Problem solved," he told her.

"In what way?"

He picked up the pace, slightly jogging, the bags bouncing on his hard back. But, as long as she could keep up, he would keep going. "Ryker got us a boat." The relief on her face made him realize just how hard this was on her. "Like I said," he said, flashing her a grin, "it'll be okay."

"Maybe," she said, "but I'm not so sure about that."

As soon as he met up with Ryker, Asher could see her spirits pick up again. He looked at her. "You were just afraid we would lose Ryker."

"I don't want to lose anybody else," she admitted. "And I still won't believe that they've got the twins until I see them."

"And that's another part of this that I don't like," he said. "They had no business not giving you that peace of mind either."

"I know," she said. "I don't like anything about this anymore."

They were now all on a small fishing boat. He looked at it and said, "This is the same one we had before."

Ryker nodded. "I had it brought to the city."

"Good thinking," Mickie said. "Can you get us back to the base?"

"No, but we can use it to intercept another boat."

"Fine," she said, as she sagged down so she was mostly hidden. "Let's get the hell out of here."

Asher looked at Ryker. "Was that the police coming in the hotel?"

"Military," he said. "Chinese military."

Asher winced. "Great. I wonder if they were looking for us specifically."

"I don't know," he said. "I sure as hell wouldn't hang around though."

"But you don't know if they were looking for us or not," she said. "Maybe it was nothing."

"No, but chances were, it was either us or Chandra. And Chandra is long gone, so it won't leave too many people to question."

"True," she said. "It still sucks though."

"What part?" Ryker said.

"All those dead bodies. Somebody has to pay for that."

"Don't worry. As soon as we get this figured out, we'll send lots of evidence and leads to the military police via our own government," he said.

"Yes, but we shouldn't have left them."

"They've already been collected," he said quietly. "That's the least of our problems right now."

As soon as they were away from most of the shipping boats, almost bouncing off each other, he turned on the engine, and they picked up a little bit of speed, heading out toward open water.

"We still have to go really slow, won't we?" she asked.

Ryker nodded. "To keep up appearances."

"But," Asher said, "a speedboat's up ahead." As they headed out, the speedboat came toward them. Asher nodded. "That's more our style."

It was a Zodiac but converted for the massive engine on its back. He came around on the shore side, and they quickly helped Mickie over, tossed in their bags, and then put out a call to have the other boat picked up. The Zodiac pulled away, and they left the fishing boat floating in the ocean.

"Is that wise?" she asked.

Ryker tapped her shoulder and pointed to the far side. "You see that little fishing boat coming toward us?"

She nodded. "I can see at least a couple of them though."

"One of them will pick up the boat and take it back in for us."

"Okay," she said in relief, "because that's in the shipping lanes. Here, you can't just leave something like that floating around."

"It's also too valuable to sink."

She turned to look at the guy manning the Zodiac. "And who's he?"

Ryker smiled and shook his head.

She groaned. More secrets. There were always secrets with these men. But, several hours later, she found herself approaching a big USS cruiser in the harbor, and she smiled. "Are we going on board?"

"Just for the moment," he said. "The last thing we want to do is put the base on alert."

"Well, why go then?" she asked.

"Because they're heading out to do a round, and we'll intercept with another ship."

She stared at him. He shrugged, smiled, and, before long, she clambered onto the big cruiser, though not a word was spoken to them or by them. She was led down to a small room, and the door was closed. This time she was alone, until Asher opened the door and stepped in behind her quickly.

"Okay," he said. "It's just the two of us here for right now."

"How long?" she asked as she walked to the closest bunk and sagged down.

He could see her wilting once again. "For a few hours."

She looked up at him with a sharp glance and asked, "Are we talking two, four, or twelve hours?"

His grin slipped to the side. "Closer to eight then. We haven't left yet, and we're heading out to open waters as part of their rounds. They're checking the area for a new game they're playing, so I'll say six to possibly eight."

"Is there any chance of food?"

"Food, coffee, water, and potentially a shower. We have your gear too."

Her eyes lit up. "In that case, let me start with a shower while you find food."

"Will do," he said, and then he hesitated.

She motioned at him. "Go on. I won't leave. I'll have a shower, and, if you're not here when I come out, I'll lie down and have a nap."

"Good enough," he said. "I could be an hour."

"Lock the door then," she said.

"I'll show you how to do it," he said, "so that I can get in again." He showed her quickly how to lock it, and then he disappeared with a hard kiss. As he headed out, he warned her. "I'll be back. Please do not step out of this room."

She smiled up at him and said, "Do you promise to come back?"

He grinned. "Absolutely I promise." And, with a second kiss, this one much gentler, he said, "I might even come back a little early."

"Well, I'll be coming out of the shower in about fifteen minutes," she said, her voice dropping. "You could always be in bed waiting for me." She waggled her eyebrows and then slammed the door in his face.

With a big bark of laughter, he headed down to take care of business. But, in his mind, he wondered if he could make that as fast as possible because the thought she had just put in his head would take a hell of a lot to get rid of.

CHAPTER 17

T HE SHOWER WAS nirvana, even though she'd been warned that there were rules for onboard showers. She didn't have the joy of a long shower, but still soap and water were a luxury which she appreciated right now. By the time she came out and dressed in clean underwear, she thought her world had suddenly brightened to become magical. She took the time to brush her teeth, to scrub her face extrahard, and to brush her hair out in front of a mirror.

It had been nothing but a nightmare for hours—for days. She was so grateful that the twins were safe, even though she hadn't had any confirmation. She planned on thinking positive that their brother did not have something to do with it and that the twins were back and that everybody had headed to Switzerland.

It was probably too soon for them to have landed in Switzerland yet, but Mickie would love to hear from them to confirm that they were home okay. She was already detaching from them and the job. It had obviously been a short-term position in her life, and she needed it at the time, but, boy, she didn't need this now. And, if Chandra was staying home, the twins wouldn't need Mickie either.

When she finally stepped from the small bathroom, her towel hung up over the door, she was disappointed to see she was alone. But she headed to the small bunk, pulled back the blankets, and, in just her underwear and bra, curled up under the sheet. The place was warm, and she really needed time to destress.

She laid here, thinking about all the things that had happened and how uncertain her future was, but she knew just how damn grateful she was to be with Asher and Ryker right now. It's not what Mickie had expected when Chandra had contacted her to join these guys in the search for the twins—neither was Mickie's last conversation with Chandra. But then, what else was new?

Mickie's life had been one endless roller coaster ride since her grandmother's death. And that brought tears to her eyes again. "I'm so sorry, Grandma," she whispered. "I wish we had so many more years together." She tugged the pillow so that she could wrap her arms around it and curled up. She was just about asleep when the door opened. She rolled over to see Asher walking in. "No food?"

He shook his head. "It's coming, but it'll be about an hour."

"Good," she said with a yawn. "I'll have a nap then."

"Or …" he said, his voice suggestive.

She froze and slowly rolled over, then looked up at him and said, "You're wearing too many clothes for that."

He dropped down beside the bunk and stared at her. "I don't want to go in this direction if you don't mean it."

She reached up and cupped his cheek. "I always meant it. I was just a little misguided back then."

He leaned over and kissed her gently, his tongue sliding between her lips to tangle with her tongue.

She loved that about him. He always gave her a chance to pull back and to say no. But she didn't want to. She looped her arms around him and tugged him closer. "You're still wearing too many clothes," she whispered as she gently traced the outline of his bottom lip before taking it in between her teeth and sucking gently.

He gave a muffled exclamation and bolted upright and quickly stripped.

"Any chance we have Ryker coming?"

He shook his head. "No, not immediately."

"Do you want to lock the door just to be sure?" He grinned, reached over, and locked the door. "He'll text before he comes anyway."

"That's very considerate of him," she said.

"Well, I think he has a pretty good idea we were headed to this reunion."

She stared at him. "How could he? I didn't even know."

"Ryker is very astute," he said. "And he already saw what was going on between us."

Then she remembered the conversation she'd overheard in the car. "I guess, but it's an interesting world right now."

"It is," he said. "And it's all ahead of you, waiting."

"I think so," she said. "I don't know what's going on with the twins and with Chandra, but I sure hope it's all good."

And that's when he stood before her completely naked. She swept off the sheets, slipped her legs over the side, and stood. He studied her bra and panties. "It looks like you're the one who's overdressed," he said, his fingers slipping under the lace of her panties. He slid his finger all the way from one hip to the other, her belly sucking in tight toward her backbone.

She whispered, "Well, you can do the honors if you want."

He smiled. "You were always good with that."

"With what?" she teased.

"Wearing just one or two pieces, enough to tantalize and to excite me, and yet, to keep everything covered." He dropped to his knees and planted a kiss on her belly button. She gasped as his hand hooked on to the elastic band, and he slowly lowered it, with his lips trailing down to the crevice and the soft curly hair hiding the most intimate part of her. She stepped out of her panties, her breath coming in rapid gasps. "You were always so damn good at that," she whispered.

He chuckled and kissed her once more, then slowly moved his way up, kissing her ribs, the softest skin between them, and up to her breastbone, where he came up against the bra. "I never did like these things," he said.

"Maybe not," she said. "But, with all the running around we've been doing, they're invaluable." She reached behind her back and quickly unhooked it. And then slowly, while he watched, she let it drop down her arms.

He took it and tossed it onto the floor with her undies and sat back on his heels, staring up at her. "You always were a goddess," he muttered, his voice thick.

She reached out, her fingers sliding through his hair as she dropped down beside him. "No, but thank you for saying that."

He chuckled. "Don't thank me," he said. "You are amazing."

She settled on her knees before him, kissed him gently and again and again. He slipped his hands down her thighs, up and around, cupping her cheeks to hold her close and sliding her thighs apart so that he could wrap her tighter around him. She shifted, rising and then lowering until his erection was tucked up between her thighs. He gasped as her thighs tightened around it.

"That's playing with fire," he murmured.

"I think fire is what we have right now," she said. "No way I'll go slow this time."

"Good," he said, his voice husky and raw. "I've wanted this for so damn long."

"Then take it," she whispered. "Take me now."

He shook his head. "Not that fast," he said, and he lowered his lips to her mouth, teasing kisses from the corner of her mouth down to her cheek and her chin, down her neck to her collarbone, licking and tasting, his hands busy circling and squeezing and cupping her buttocks and holding her tight. He slid one finger down the crack between them, feeling her surge up against him. And then, when she surged up, he picked her up slightly and lifted her higher so he could take one plump breast into his mouth and suckle hard. The nipple hardened fast, and he moved from one to the other, laving the tips incessantly.

She twisted in his arms. "Dammit," she said. "I need you."

"I know," he said, sliding one finger between the lips to spread the moisture of her desire to make his entry easier. And then, even still on his knees, he slowly lowered her onto his shaft. Her thighs wrapped around his waist until she was basically impaled on his shaft.

She opened her eyes. "Good God."

He smiled. But he cupped her buttocks and lifted her ever-so-slightly and then lowered her, and she caught on. With her arms looped around his neck, she started to ride, slow and steady, their lips fused together as their bodies, from hips to collarbone, melded to match the heat driving from within. She gasped and murmured as she sped up, twisting in his arms as he struggled to keep her close. Once he held her tight, his hips pistoned back and forth. Once, twice, three times. She shifted, trying to change positions, but he held her still tighter as he drove deeper and deeper and deeper, and finally his body exploded in shudders. As she felt his climax race upon him, it sent her over the edge too. And she laid still in his lap and tried to recover.

Finally he grabbed the top bunk with one hand, his other arm firmly around her, and, still inside her, stood, and laid them both gently on the lower bunk, their bodies fused together. And just as she thought that maybe he would remove himself to lie down beside her, he started to drive again.

She cried out in an instant as she went from zero to sixty, and her body wrapped around his, twisting and climbing his frame, screaming once again as she exploded with her own orgasm. He followed her down this time and collapsed beside her.

She shuddered as she laid there. "Well, the first was wow," she murmured. "But the second? ... That was crazy."

ASHER CHUCKLED AT her last comment. But Mickie was right. It was freaking awesome. He held her close and whispered, "Do you want to nap while I have a quick shower?"

"After that, I feel like I should have one too," she murmured.

"Well, food will be here soon," he said.

Her eyes flew open, and she looked up at him and said, "Maybe you go first, and then I'll whip in and have a quick one afterward."

So he hopped up, quickly ran through his normal shower routine, and stepped out with a towel wrapped around his hips and then dressed in fresh clothes. As soon as he was out, she dashed in and quickly cleaned up again. He made the bed, but that sultry smell in the air was unmistakable. He shrugged. There wasn't a whole lot he could do about it.

Just then Ryker knocked on the door and said, "Mickie, Ryker is here." Asher opened the door to see Ryker with a trolley full of trays laden with food. He pushed in the trolley and said, "It's enough for the three of us."

"Good. Do you have any updates?"

Ryker shook his head. "No, but we're leaving port anytime now. There's a bit of excitement at the Shanghai Naval Base though."

"Great," he said. "Are they looking for us?"

Ryker nodded. "It appears so."

"It would be really nice if we'd get out of port then."

Just then they heard the engines start up. He looked at Ryker and smiled. "Good," he said. "The sooner we get on to the next step, the better."

"Has she heard anything from Chandra?"

Just then Mickie came out of the bathroom, her face clean and her hair moist around her face. She was dressed in clean clothes, and she said in a calm voice, "No." Her eyes lit on seeing the trolley. "Food," she cried out.

Ryker laughed. "Yes, food. Come and eat."

She immediately hung her towel back up and stepped closer to take a look at what there was. "Oh my," she said. "This is like real food. Not a sandwich in sight."

He laughed. "We've got pork chops, broccoli, veggies, and some rice. It's all here."

"Perfect," she said. It was a little awkward with the bunks filling this small room, but that didn't stop anybody from collecting a plateful of food and sitting back down again. As soon as she was done with her first serving, she looked to see if there were any leftovers and then helped herself.

"Sorry, guys," she said, shifting back so she leaned against the wall. "I didn't realize how hungry I was."

"That's what it's here for," Asher said. "Now maybe we can get to the bottom of all this mess."

"Can I go home now?" she asked. "And, of course, I feel terrible about that because I still haven't had confirmation of the twins."

"I hear you," he said. "But, with any luck, that's in progress, and we'll get word soon."

"You do realize it's quite possible they've all been kidnapped?" Mickie asked.

"I know," Asher said, "but we do have confirmation that a private jet left Shanghai with four passengers on board. They filed a flight plan to Switzerland."

"Great," she said, some of her feelings showing on her face.

"It's okay," he said. "We'll get to Geneva soon."

"How soon?"

He shrugged. "We'll be there tomorrow."

She thought about it, then nodded. "Okay. It'd probably be half a day traveling by air anyways."

"Yeah, I checked. Thirteen to fifteen hours on a commercial flight, as there is no direct shot there. Unless, of course, they are taking a private jet," he said. "Remember. We're trying to avoid any public railways and cameras."

"Exactly."

And, with that, she finished off her plate and poured herself a cup of coffee and sagged into the corner.

As he caught sight of her eyes closing and her head tilting sideways, he grabbed the cup she held. She looked at him, blurry-eyed, and asked, "Did I drink it?"

"You did," he lied. "Lie down and sleep."

She curled up in the corner and was out. He returned her almost full cup to the trolley and looked at Ryker, who had a grin on his face.

"Looks like things are much better in paradise."

"Much," Asher said.

"She'll handle this lifestyle?"

"Well, apparently neither of us were doing all that great apart. So hopefully together we can at least be just as bad," he joked.

"You'll be fine," Ryker said. "But she's got the right idea. Let's finish up, and then we can both crash."

They quickly finished off the food, and, this time, Asher took the trolley outside and locked it into place a few feet from the dumbwaiter. It would be picked up very quickly, he knew. Back inside, Ryker was already stretched out in the opposite bunk. Asher noted Mickie had stretched out and covered most of the bottom bunk, so he quickly crawled up onto the top bunk and stretched out.

The best thing he could do was sleep. It would be a crazy few hours as soon as they disembarked. But it was all good. For the first time in a long time, he felt pretty damn fine about everything.

CHAPTER 18

W HEN THEY'D SAID that they would be in Geneva the next day, what they hadn't mentioned was that they were moving from the cruiser to a warship to a helicopter to another warship and then to an international US airstrip to catch a military flight into Switzerland. Once in Geneva, they rented a vehicle and headed toward the home that Mickie had occupied for the last six months. As she came up to the gates, they were closed. "Is it safe to return here?"

Asher nodded.

"But this is the lion's den."

Asher smiled, but Ryker spoke this time. "We've got backup in place here."

Still worried but trusting these men, she hopped out and hit the button on the side. "Hey, Leonard," she said to the security guard on duty. "Can you let me in?"

"Hey, Mickie, nice to see you back again." He pushed the button.

Before she hopped back into the car, she asked, "Everybody home safe and sound?"

"Yep, safe as can be."

When she got back into the car, she said, "According to Leonard, everybody's here."

"Interesting," they said, and they drove up to the front doors.

"So we're allowed inside. That's a good sign, right?" Mickie asked.

The men shared a knowing look.

"Or … it's a trap?"

Asher winked. "We've got this covered."

She was still trying to shake out the weird feeling from all the different travel modes. And it certainly worked in the sense that nobody would have seen her face, but was that a good thing? As they walked up to the front steps, she asked, "Have you guys had any updates yet from Chandra?"

"No, but our people confirm that the Chinese military is cooperating with the local authorities as to the dead left behind," he said. "And they're pretty pissed because they figured that they lost the one key person involved in the murders."

"And what about Lana?"

"Oh, that's what's new," Ryker said. "She turned up dead."

At the top step, Mickie froze and turned to look at him. "Seriously?"

"Yes. Supposedly a hit-and-run," he said in a wry tone. "Nobody has any details."

"Great," she said as she entered the big doors of the mansion.

Edward's head of security walked toward her. All six foot eight of him. "And what are you doing here?" he asked suspiciously.

She stared at him. "So, is Edward taking over this place too then?" she asked lightly.

He frowned and said, "I must let them know you're here."

"I live here," she snapped.

He stiffened, and his head reared. "Well, I don't know about that anymore." He turned and headed toward the living room.

Not to be outdone, she followed on his heels. Chandra sat beside the fire, even though a hot summer day. She looked up in shock when she saw Mickie. Chandra jumped to her feet and came over. "Oh, am I glad to see you," she said. "We didn't know what had happened to you."

"You mean, after you canceled my hotel room and didn't give me a flight home?" she asked, desperately trying to hold back the bitterness.

Chandra looked at her in shock. "I never canceled your hotel room."

"The day you left," she said, "my room was already given away to another customer, and they were told that I wouldn't be back. And my room wasn't paid for and then you never contacted me with my flight information."

"Edward took care of that," Chandra said.

Mickie turned to see Edward standing by the window. "Yeah, Edward, did you?" Mickie said in a mocking tone.

Edward looked at her like he always had, as if she were some foreign bug.

She remembered when he had first met her and had called her an American. There had been such disgust in his voice. He had been born somewhere in Europe and felt himself above his mother and his twin sisters, who had all been born in America as well.

"It must have been a mistake or a clerical error or something," he said with a shrug. He turned to look at the two men with her, and his gaze turned hostile. "And who are they?"

Ryker and Asher both crossed their arms over their

chests and stared back at him blandly.

"They're the men who helped me in China to get home again," she said. Then she turned to look at Chandra. "They're also the men who found the twins for you, and you just ran out on us."

"Oh, my dear, I'm so sorry, but I had the twins, and I had to get them home."

"You wouldn't even take me with you," she said. "Neither would you tell me that the twins were okay. I spent days in China trying to find them. Have you forgotten that I was also injured in that kidnapping mess?"

Chandra didn't grasp the significance of what she'd done—but then she lived in a world where, with a snap of her fingers, she could have anything and everything she wanted. She motioned at the seat beside her. "Sit down. You must be tired."

"I am," Mickie said, yawning. "It's been a pretty rough trip."

"And how did you fly home?" Edward asked.

She glanced at him and glared. "Not the normal way," she said. "Why? Were you paying people to find out when I entered the country?"

He made a hand motion as if to say it wasn't worth his time. "I hear there was quite a mess in China," he said.

"There was," she said. "I wonder how much of it was your doing."

At that, his face turned to a dark scowl. "There will be no more of that talk from you."

Chandra herself reached out and grasped Mickie's hands. "I don't know what you've heard, but Edward didn't have anything to do with this."

"No, of course not," she said. She glanced at Asher and

Ryker and shrugged. It's not like she knew how to handle this scenario. She faced Chandra. "What about the twins? Are they okay?"

Chandra smiled. "They are."

"And what came of all this mess about a wedding that you're supposed to do for somebody and paying out five million dollars so that you can get your daughters back?" Asher asked, his voice hard.

Chandra looked completely dumbfounded at that. "I don't know," she said. "It all went to hell. Then Edward stepped in, and got them back. For which I am forever grateful."

"And just like that, less than an hour later, you leave the country," Mickie said.

"I can see that you're upset, dear," Chandra said, getting a little upset herself. "And it's really not my fault. Obviously I had to put the twins' care first."

Mickie nodded. "Of course you did." But her gaze never left Chandra's son.

Edward looked like this whole thing was completely beneath him.

"May I see them?"

"Of course you can," she said. "They'll be here in a few minutes anyway."

"Are they recovered from the drugs?"

Chandra nodded. "So good of you to worry. They'll be fine."

Just then footsteps were outside. The doors opened again and in came Amelia and Alisha. When they saw Mickie, their faces lit up. Mickie raced toward the two beautiful women, engulfing them in hugs. The three of them stood, talking back and forth incessantly. She stepped back and looked up at them, her hand holding one of each of theirs. "I'm so happy you're safe."

"Of course they're safe," Edward said. "We aren't telling them all the nasty details. What they don't know won't hurt them."

Mickie ignored him, asking the twins, "Do you remember who kidnapped you?"

Both of the women immediately nodded.

"Do you remember your old nanny?"

Alicia nodded. "Yes, Lana was there.'

"Yes, she was, wasn't she?" Mickie said, laughing. She hugged the first one again and then the other. "I'm so happy that you're safe at home." Then she walked with them to the couch. And she turned to see Edward frozen in place and Chandra standing stiff, staring at her.

"What was that about their ex-nanny?" Chandra asked.

"You didn't know?" Mickie asked. "Didn't Edward tell you?" She turned to Edward. "Why didn't you tell your mother that Wilson Chang, her marketing guru, and his sister, Lana, the twins' former nanny, were involved in the *original* kidnapping? Because obviously you would have told Chandra if you knew, right? But then again you were also involved, so whatever, right?"

He almost spat he was so mad. He stormed to stand in front of her.

Immediately Asher stepped up beside her.

He looked at him and glared. "What? You bring your watchdog in here?"

"Well, we brought a whole lot more than one watchdog," she said.

"What are you talking about?" Chandra asked. "Edward didn't have anything to do with this. I told you that. And, if that bitch Lana did, well, that makes a whole lot of sense. She was always trouble."

Mickie looked at her. "She worked for you for ten years."

"And damn near had the twins convinced that she was their mother too."

"And that's why she was kidnapping them. Because she didn't want to live without them," Mickie said gently. "At least that was how it started."

"Well, wait until I have a talk with that girl," Chandra said, completely affronted. "They're *my* daughters."

Mickie nodded slowly. "Yes, but, because you were always gone, and Lana spent so much time with them, she felt like they were hers."

"I don't care. She had no business doing that. Wait until I speak with her."

"That'll be a little hard to do," Asher said. "She was murdered yesterday."

At that, Chandra stared at him, her jaw dropping. "What?"

"Yeah, funny how that happens," he said. "She was in a hit-and-run accident."

She shook her head. "I don't understand."

"No," he said. "There's a lot you don't understand. Is your marketing guru here? I'm sure he would like to know about his sister's demise."

She looked at Edward. "Can you call him in, please?"

Edward nodded and walked around to the desk, then punched in a code for the PA system overhead. He schooled his voice as he called Wilson into the main drawing room. They waited in silence, but nobody arrived.

"When did you last see him?" Mickie asked Chandra.

"When we arrived, but I haven't seen much of him since."

"Today at all?"

Chandra shook her head. Then she looked at Edward. "Edward, have you seen him today?"

"I don't think so, no," he said. "Why?"

"Well, now that his sister has passed on, and he was involved in this plot from the beginning," Mickie said, "you might want to make sure that he's captured."

"Says you," Edward said with a sneer.

"So says the US government and the Chinese government," she said smoothly. "So I highly suggest that somebody find him and fast. Otherwise, of course, we'll phone for the Swiss military to come in and pick him up."

"I don't understand what's going on," Chandra said, looking dazed. "Why would Wilson do that?"

"Well, more than that, I'm pretty sure he's responsible for the related murders in China," Mickie said. But, once again, she didn't take her gaze off Edward.

Chandra gasped, her hand on her chest. "But this is awful. Somebody please explain what's going on."

"It's quite simple," Asher said, wrapping an arm around Mickie's shoulder and holding her close. "Your old nanny, Lana, wanted to keep the twins with her. The six months that she was away from them was just too much. Her brother, Wilson, persuaded you to take the twins to China, where he helped his sister kidnap them. Only somebody got wind of it and decided that it would be a perfect opportunity for him to make a knight-in-shining-armor appearance and save the day. Hence, your son, Edward. So you see, they're all involved."

Chandra stared at Asher for a long moment; then her

gaze went from Mickie to Edward and then back to Asher. Her bottom lip trembled. "Surely that can't be."

"Of course it is," Mickie said. "Just think about all the stories we were told and all the chaos and the confusion. It was smoke and mirrors. All of it was smoke and mirrors. But, in the meantime, a lot of people lost their lives. More than I even care to remember." She sat here in silence, thinking about even the fisherman and his family, whose only crime was to offer his boat to hold the twins. In a surprise move, she turned on Edward and said, "Did you kill the fisherman too?"

"I didn't kill anybody," he snapped.

"Interesting," she said. "Because the nurse who helped with the twins initially is dead. And we've got her two brothers in jail. They were the second set of kidnappers. But the two gunmen, who were the initial kidnappers, they are dead too. Plus Lana is dead, and the fisherman is dead, and his family is all dead in the fire set at their home. All dead. How many others did we forget about or do we not even know of?" she asked, fatigue in her voice.

"And we've got the lovely marketing guru, Wilson Chang, who is either dead or the next one to die. And all for what, Edward? Just because you wanted your mother's attention? Or because you wanted your sisters' trust fund?"

"I don't know what you're talking about," he said. "You're obviously overwrought. I don't know what kind of nonsense Lana filled your head with, but that woman was certifiable and obviously dangerous. She needed to be fired. It was completely unacceptable to fill the twins' heads with all that garbage."

The twins sat on the couch, their arms wrapped around each other, their gazes going from one speaker to the other.

Mickie got up, walked over, and sat down beside them. "It'll be okay," she said. "I'm sorry you had to hear all this."

"Sweng brought us back," one of the twins said. "He took us to the hotel."

"Of course he did," Chandra said. "Once we found out where you were, he's the one who went to get you, along with Edward."

The twins nodded. "Lana was there too."

Chandra got up and joined the twins, then crouched in front of her daughters and said, "It won't happen again. I'll cut back on all my appointments, and I'll stay home now."

The twins' faces lit up, and the three of them shared a hug.

Mickie joined Asher and asked, "Now what?"

"I guess it depends," he said. "Depends on how much of a clean sweep comes from this."

A new voice entered the fray. "There won't be one," Wilson said, as he entered from the side door. He had two handguns. "This is absolutely ridiculous. You can't retire. That's my job you are ending!"

She stared at him in affront. "You always knew I would retire in a few years. What are you doing with those guns? Put them away, for heaven's sake."

He shook his head slowly. "It's my career that you're killing."

"No, you can work for anybody else," she said. "What did you think I would do? Keep working forever?"

He stared up at the ceiling, looking for patience. "No, not forever, but you had to at least get me to the point where I was established and where I had all those contacts."

"You do have them," she said. "It's got nothing to do with you whether I quit or not."

"Yes, it does," he said. "Because I'll always be known as your assistant."

"Well, I can give you references, for heaven's sake," she said.

"But I won't make that kind of money."

"What kind of money?" she asked, frowning.

"Well, they had to pay the deposit for your services, but they had to bribe me to even get on the damn list."

She stared at him in shock. "What?"

"Yes," he said. "Your deposit was half a million, but they were paying me half of that again."

Everybody stared at him. "That's a lot of money," Asher said in a calm voice.

"It is. But still, you were talking about retiring anyway," he said. "Lana wanted the twins. I told her it was a stupid idea, but then she told me about the trust fund, and I realized that it wasn't such a stupid idea. Whoever had control of the twins had the trust fund, so she wanted to kidnap them, where she could look after them like she always had."

He turned to Chandra and sneered. "You call yourself their mother. You may have given birth to them, but you've done nothing but be ashamed of them ever since. You've hidden them away and locked them up so nobody could even see them. My sister brought them into the modeling world. You didn't want anybody to know that they were yours because they're weren't perfect."

Chandra's face paled, but she straightened and held her shoulders stiff. "I won't listen to your lies or your nastiness."

"No, you may not want to listen," he said, "but I'm the one with the gun, so you'll listen as much as I want you to." Chang looked at Edward. "Edward got wind of what happened though," he said.

Then Chang turned to Mickie. "You were right. Edward wanted to ride in as the white knight and to rescue the twins from everything. Of course, it cost him more than he'll know because we had to take out quite a few people to do this. It was typical of Lana to have half-baked ideas. I don't even know how many men she killed. But she had to be taken out as well because she wouldn't agree to bring back the twins.

"But I knew that there was no way the models would stay hidden like that, even with Lana's wild idea to buy an island for her and them. And once Edward got involved and agreed to pay me a nice sum of money so that I could retire, I agreed for him to return the twins. But Lana fought me on it. She was furious. She didn't want anything to do with letting them go. So, well, she had to be removed."

"You killed your sister because she wouldn't agree to return the twins?" Ryker shook his head. "You're all just greedy little bastards."

Wilson looked at him and said, "You're a nobody. We had you running all over the town. We kicked you loose each and every time."

"Not quite," Asher said. "We're here, aren't we?"

"Sure, and so what?" he said. "It's not like anybody's with you. Nobody gives a shit. I'll just deep-six the three of you, and nobody will know."

"*Three* of us?" Mickie asked, stepping toward him. "What about Edward? What about Chandra? What about the twins?"

"Well, Edward, I don't have to shoot," he said. "He'll just pay me to go away, and that's fine. Chandra will pay me to go away too. And the twins? … Well, if I kill them, I don't know what happens to the trust fund. I must figure that out first."

"So, there's only one easy answer then," Ryker said, walking toward him.

"Whoa, whoa, stop where you are," he said, lifting his hand. "I'll shoot you right where you stand."

"You might," Ryker said, "but you've got to be fast enough." He dropped to the floor and his foot kicked Wilson to the ground with a hard *thunk*, one handgun flying.

Ryker then picked up the second handgun and said, "That takes care of that."

Mickie looked at him in shock, running to Ryker's side. "You didn't kill him, did you?"

"I told you that we don't arbitrarily kill anyone," Asher said. "Just these little assholes do that. They can't figure out any other way."

And, as one, they turned to look at Edward.

He shrugged and said, "What did I do exactly? I rescued the twins from him."

"And, of course, you were going to tell your mother all about it, right?" Mickie said in a dry tone.

"The less she has to deal with, the better," he said. "This has been a particularly stressful time for her."

Mickie snorted at that. "You think?" Then she glanced back at Asher. "What do you think? Did he do anything wrong?"

"I highly doubt the Chinese police care about him," he said, "providing he didn't kill anybody."

"I didn't kill anybody," he snorted. "I told you that I found out what was going on. I made arrangements, and I rescued my sisters." He walked over to his mother and dropped his hand on her shoulder. "And this is family business, and, since none of you are family, please leave now." He glanced at Mickie and said, "And obviously you're fired."

"Oh, absolutely," she said. "I'll sell this story to the tabloids."

Chandra gasped in dismay. She hopped to her feet and said, "That's not fair."

"Neither is dumping me in China, probably so all the murders were hung on me," Mickie said. She hadn't meant a word about selling the story to the tabloids. She just wanted something to shove into insufferable Edward's face. "After everything I went through, you leave me there without looking after me? You haven't paid me my wages, and you owe me a severance," she snapped. "I know you are in trouble financially, Edward, but you still owe me."

Edward's nostrils flared.

She nodded. "I do have a contract. And, if you think I won't push for what's rightly coming to me," she said, "you're wrong. And then I'll sit down, and I'll talk to the police and see if we can hang anything around your neck. Because, at the very least, you've dropped a litter of bodies behind you." As she walked toward the door with the men on either side of her, she stopped and turned. "How did you get the twins' drugged bodies out of those two boats?"

"What are you talking about?" he asked. "Wilson got them."

"No, you were there," she said, remembering the face that she recognized along with Lana's. "You three were all there at the same time."

Edward shrugged. "Sure, but I didn't go out after the twins. Wilson did."

"Alone?"

"Of course alone," he said in exaggeration.

And that's when she stopped, looked at him, and smiled. "And now you're lying. Because nobody alone could have carried each of those twins off the two boats onto shore. Not only that, but he piloted one boat back to shore, and you piloted the other."

"There was the guy from the other boat," he said swiftly. But he shuffled uneasily.

And she shook her head. "No, no," she said. "You were there and helped him to carry the drugged sisters from the boat to the crossover vehicle. The boat driver couldn't have done it alone. And then, when that was done, Wilson killed the fisherman."

"That's what I said."

She looked up at Asher, who was grinning at Edward. "And that makes you a murderer," he said. "Because you were part of the team who killed him. And then there's the house fire that took out the poor fisherman's family."

"I didn't kill him. I was trying to rescue my sisters. Nobody will charge me for rescuing my sisters."

"Well, I'm not so sure about that," Mickie said. "We'll see what the Chinese police say." And she turned and walked out, closing the doors behind her.

Edward could be heard yelling and screaming on the other side of the doors.

As she headed to the front door, Chandra came running behind her. "Please, please don't say anything," she wailed. "It's been tough enough already."

She turned to look at Chandra. "What about that fisherman's family? Awan Hania and his entire family were wiped out. Did you know about that?" she asked. "Do you realize Wilson and Edward burned the family in their own home to the ground? Mother, father, sister? Do you think Wilson did that alone? No, it was the two of them each and every step of the way. And likely Sweng as added assistance. They hired gunmen to kidnap the twins, then killed the gunmen," she cried in outrage. "And, believe me, when Wilson wakes up, he'll confirm it. Your son needs eighty million dollars to keep his construction business alive. He is only after the twins' money—their trust fund—don't you get that?"

Chandra looked at her, her face twisted in fury. "Don't you understand? None of that's important. None of it. What was important was getting my girls back."

"And why is that? Lana was right. For decades, you never even saw the twins, according to the diaries I read."

"But I know how wrong that was," she said eagerly. "I understand that now. And I'm trying to change it. I'll be a good mom now."

"And a lot of people," she said, "a lot of people lost their lives because of your son."

"No," Chandra said. "Again you misunderstand. My son did a good thing. He saved his sisters."

"And I suppose you'll go to any lengths in order to keep him out of prison."

"Of course," she said in surprise. "He's my son. He's not going to prison."

"Well, we'll see," she said.

Ryker opened the front door and let the Swiss militia in, while Asher showed her his phone, the red recording light lit.

"What are they doing here?" Chandra cried out in horror, then rage, as the men marched past her toward where Edward stood.

"Well, I suppose they'll start with taking the two men in

for questioning, then will come extradition proceedings. Charges, a trial, and then prison," Mickie said. "So you better find the best lawyer money can buy because your son'll need it." She stepped out the front door as Chandra pivoted to follow the two military men headed into the room to collect their two prisoners. Mickie took several breaths of fresh air. "I will miss the twins."

"They didn't look like they had much to say on the couch."

"Often, when in situations like this, they just lock down inside," she said sadly. "They'll need help. Maybe if Chandra is there for them, that will get them through this, but I don't know."

"Do you feel like you need to be here?"

"It doesn't matter," she said. "My time with this family is over. And I'm pretty confident they'll ensure I don't ever get a chance to see them again."

"Probably," he said.

As they stood there, Edward and Wilson were brought out by the military.

Chandra stood on the front steps. "I'll meet you at the station. I've called our lawyers," Chandra called out.

Edward lifted a hand in acknowledgment.

Chandra turned to Mickie. "I know you don't think that I appreciate what you went through, and I really am sorry that you seem to have been dropped in the middle of nowhere at the end of it."

"*Right*," Mickie said, not sure she believed a word out of the older woman's mouth.

But Chandra held out an envelope and her hand to shake. "Here's your pay, as agreed to in our contract, and I've reimbursed you for the flight and the hotel in China, as well as a little bit extra for your troubles. I know I can't stop you from selling your story or doing anything else related to these horrid events, but I hope you realize that our family has been through enough strife and ask that maybe you show a little respect for our troubles too."

A man delivered several suitcases and placed them on the front step.

"Here are Mickie's belongings." And then, with a stiff nod at the three of them, she turned and walked back inside, closing the door with a hard *snick*.

Mickie glanced up at Asher and Ryker and said, "Well, that's over with." She dropped the envelope into her purse.

"You're not opening it?"

She shook her head. "No, it'll be whatever it'll be. I'm more than ready to walk away from this chapter of my life." She would miss the twins, but she could do only so much, and she couldn't deal with this. She walked down the rest of the steps and headed back to the car. "What are you guys doing right now?"

"Well, I'm heading back to the US," Ryker said. "Asher, what are you doing?"

"Well, you know what? I haven't spent any time in Geneva for a while. I think I'll spend a few days here."

She glanced at him and smiled. "You want a houseguest? Or do you want to join me at my grandmother's house? I inherited it."

He nodded. "I'd be delighted. Let's grab your bags." He looked at Ryker. "Can you give us a lift?"

"For you two, anything."

And that's what they did. They quickly grabbed all her personal possessions and her tote bag, then loaded it into the car. Nobody said a word, and she never saw anybody as they left the grounds. She turned and watched as they headed out the gate.

"Will you be okay?" Asher asked her.

"I'll be better than okay," she said. "It's just sad in a way."

"It's always sad to turn a new leaf," Asher said. "But the good thing is, we get to face forward and create a whole new future."

"Together?"

He lifted her hand and kissed the back of it gently. "If you would like to, yes."

"I'd like to," she said. "I feel like we're finally coming back around to what we were supposed to do in the first place. I just took a side street."

"And sometimes we must take those side streets," he said. "They're important for one reason or another."

"Well, as long as I've got it together now," she said. Then she leaned up and kissed him. "I like the sound of *together.*"

"Me too," he said and kissed her back.

EPILOGUE

RYKER LANDERS STAYED an extra night in Geneva and spent it with Mickie and Asher. They went out for dinner, sat at the lake for a long time, and just generally had a good old time without the pressure and strain of all the action they'd been through. Ryker had no idea where he was going next, but he hoped for a few days off when he landed in California. He was heading to his brother's place now. He figured he'd catch a couple days of doing nothing but maybe playing a few video games and something mundane, like mowing the lawn. That sounded good to him. Especially if it came with a cold beer.

He hopped into his vehicle and headed away from the airport. He hated the traffic, the smell, and the smog, but there was something very comforting about being home again. As he pulled up to his brother's front door, it opened, and his nephew came barreling out.

"Uncle Ryker," he said. "You came."

"I said I would, buddy." He picked him up, tossed him high in the air, and laughed.

As he stepped inside, his sister-in-law came over and gave him a kiss. "You look tired."

"Yeah, it's been a bit of a rush," he said. "After a few days I'll be fine."

His brother, Reggie, walked over, patted his back, and

said, "Will they give you a few days?"

"I hope so," he said.

But just over a day later his phone chimed. He looked down at the screen. **You ready?**

He thought about it, smiled, and answered. **Yes. This Asher?**

Good. came the reply. **You're heading to the jungle. A geologist has gone missing.**

I could take a whole team in there and still not find him.

We think *she* has been taken by guerillas.

The animal variety? he typed, half as a bad joke.

No, the well-armed variety. We need somebody to get her out without causing a war.

But I like causing wars, Ryker typed.

Then cause it with her. She's been looking for platinum, a hot commodity in the world. We're afraid she found some—and someone else found out.

Not good.

So get ready. You're leaving in the morning.

This concludes Book 5 of The Mavericks: Asher.

Read about Ryker: The Mavericks, Book 6

The Mavericks: Ryker (Book #6)

What happens when the very men—trained to make the hard decisions—come up against the rules and regulations that hold them back from doing what needs to be done? They either stay and work within the constraints given to them or they walk away. Only now, for a select few, they have another option:

The Mavericks. A covert black ops team that steps up and break all the rules … but gets the job done.

Welcome to a new military romance series by USA Today best-selling author Dale Mayer. A series where you meet new friends and just might get to meet old ones too in this raw and compelling look at the men who keep us safe every day from the darkness where they operate—and live—in the shadows … until someone special helps them step into the light.

After his last assignment, Ryker is ready for a rest. And he gets it—but only a few hours …

That's even too long for a geologist kidnapped by guerrillas in the Columbian jungle. Ryker has plenty of experience in jungles around the world but, keeping Manila safe—along with the two men she's traveling with and their injured guide—exposes them for who they are. It quickly becomes apparent, under these most gruelling conditions, which of her party steps up and which plan to step out.

Manila's life has become one of never-ending misery at the hands of her captors as they await word from their bosses, who decide her ultimate fate. That she's hunting platinum doesn't matter to them. Nor that she's fighting against the invasive illegal gold mining taking over parts of the area. When Ryker rescues her from her prison tent, she places her trust in his ability to get her and her team safely away. Not yet realizing she'd be gifting him both her body and her heart too.

Ryker needs to keep them all alive and together long enough to get them out of this hellhole—hopefully alive ...

Find book 6 here!
To find out more visit Dale Mayer's website.
http://smarturl.it/DMRykerUniversal

Author's Note

Thank you for reading Asher: The Mavericks, Book 5! If you enjoyed the book, please take a moment and leave a short review.

Dear reader,

I love to hear from readers, and you can contact me at my website: www.dalemayer.com or at my Facebook author page. To be informed of new releases and special offers, sign up for my newsletter or follow me on BookBub. And if you are interested in joining Dale Mayer's Reader Group, here is the Facebook sign up page.
https://smarturl.it/DaleMayerFBGroup

Cheers,
Dale Mayer

Get THREE Free Books Now!

Have you met the SEALS of Honor?

SEALs of Honor Books 1, 2, and 3. Follow the stories of brave, badass warriors who serve their country with honor and love their women to the limits of life and death.

Read Mason, Hawk, and Dane right now for FREE.

Go here and tell me where to send them!
http://smarturl.it/EthanBofB

About the Author

Dale Mayer is a USA Today bestselling author best known for her Psychic Visions and Family Blood Ties series. Her contemporary romances are raw and full of passion and emotion (Second Chances, SKIN), her thrillers will keep you guessing (By Death series), and her romantic comedies will keep you giggling (It's a Dog's Life and Charmin Marvin Romantic Comedy series).

She honors the stories that come to her – and some of them are crazy and break all the rules and cross multiple genres!

To go with her fiction, she also writes nonfiction in many different fields with books available on resume writing, companion gardening and the US mortgage system. She has recently published her Career Essentials Series. All her books are available in print and ebook format.

Connect with Dale Mayer Online

Dale's Website – www.dalemayer.com

Facebook Personal – https://smarturl.it/DaleMayer

Instagram – https://smarturl.it/DaleMayerInstagram

BookBub – https://smarturl.it/DaleMayerBookbub

Facebook Fan Page – https://smarturl.it/DaleMayerFBFanPage

Goodreads – https://smarturl.it/DaleMayerGoodreads

Also by Dale Mayer

Published Adult Books:

Hathaway House
Aaron, Book 1
Brock, Book 2
Cole, Book 3
Denton, Book 4
Elliot, Book 5
Finn, Book 6
Gregory, Book 7

The K9 Files
Ethan, Book 1
Pierce, Book 2
Zane, Book 3
Blaze, Book 4
Lucas, Book 5
Parker, Book 6
Carter, Book 7

Lovely Lethal Gardens
Arsenic in the Azaleas, Book 1
Bones in the Begonias, Book 2
Corpse in the Carnations, Book 3
Daggers in the Dahlias, Book 4
Evidence in the Echinacea, Book 5
Footprints in the Ferns, Book 6

Gun in the Gardenias, Book 7
Handcuffs in the Heather, Book 8

Psychic Vision Series
Tuesday's Child
Hide 'n Go Seek
Maddy's Floor
Garden of Sorrow
Knock Knock...
Rare Find
Eyes to the Soul
Now You See Her
Shattered
Into the Abyss
Seeds of Malice
Eye of the Falcon
Itsy-Bitsy Spider
Unmasked
Deep Beneath
From the Ashes
Psychic Visions Books 1–3
Psychic Visions Books 4–6
Psychic Visions Books 7–9

By Death Series
Touched by Death
Haunted by Death
Chilled by Death
By Death Books 1–3

Broken Protocols – Romantic Comedy Series
Cat's Meow
Cat's Pajamas

Cat's Cradle
Cat's Claus
Broken Protocols 1-4

Broken and... Mending
Skin
Scars
Scales (of Justice)
Broken but... Mending 1-3

Glory
Genesis
Tori
Celeste
Glory Trilogy

Biker Blues
Morgan: Biker Blues, Volume 1
Cash: Biker Blues, Volume 2

SEALs of Honor
Mason: SEALs of Honor, Book 1
Hawk: SEALs of Honor, Book 2
Dane: SEALs of Honor, Book 3
Swede: SEALs of Honor, Book 4
Shadow: SEALs of Honor, Book 5
Cooper: SEALs of Honor, Book 6
Markus: SEALs of Honor, Book 7
Evan: SEALs of Honor, Book 8
Mason's Wish: SEALs of Honor, Book 9
Chase: SEALs of Honor, Book 10
Brett: SEALs of Honor, Book 11
Devlin: SEALs of Honor, Book 12

Easton: SEALs of Honor, Book 13
Ryder: SEALs of Honor, Book 14
Macklin: SEALs of Honor, Book 15
Corey: SEALs of Honor, Book 16
Warrick: SEALs of Honor, Book 17
Tanner: SEALs of Honor, Book 18
Jackson: SEALs of Honor, Book 19
Kanen: SEALs of Honor, Book 20
Nelson: SEALs of Honor, Book 21
Taylor: SEALs of Honor, Book 22
SEALs of Honor, Books 1–3
SEALs of Honor, Books 4–6
SEALs of Honor, Books 7–10
SEALs of Honor, Books 11–13
SEALs of Honor, Books 14–16
SEALs of Honor, Books 17–19

Heroes for Hire

Levi's Legend: Heroes for Hire, Book 1
Stone's Surrender: Heroes for Hire, Book 2
Merk's Mistake: Heroes for Hire, Book 3
Rhodes's Reward: Heroes for Hire, Book 4
Flynn's Firecracker: Heroes for Hire, Book 5
Logan's Light: Heroes for Hire, Book 6
Harrison's Heart: Heroes for Hire, Book 7
Saul's Sweetheart: Heroes for Hire, Book 8
Dakota's Delight: Heroes for Hire, Book 9
Michael's Mercy (Part of Sleeper SEAL Series)
Tyson's Treasure: Heroes for Hire, Book 10
Jace's Jewel: Heroes for Hire, Book 11
Rory's Rose: Heroes for Hire, Book 12
Brandon's Bliss: Heroes for Hire, Book 13

SEALs of Steel

The Mavericks

Miles, Book 7
Nico, Book 8
Keane, Book 9
Lennox, Book 10
Gavin, Book 11
Shane, Book 12

Collections
Dare to Be You...
Dare to Love...
Dare to be Strong...
RomanceX3

Standalone Novellas
It's a Dog's Life
Riana's Revenge
Second Chances

Published Young Adult Books:

Family Blood Ties Series
Vampire in Denial
Vampire in Distress
Vampire in Design
Vampire in Deceit
Vampire in Defiance
Vampire in Conflict
Vampire in Chaos
Vampire in Crisis
Vampire in Control
Vampire in Charge
Family Blood Ties Set 1–3
Family Blood Ties Set 1–5

Family Blood Ties Set 4–6
Family Blood Ties Set 7–9
Sian's Solution, A Family Blood Ties Series Prequel
    Novelette

Design series
Dangerous Designs
Deadly Designs
Darkest Designs
Design Series Trilogy

Standalone
In Cassie's Corner
Gem Stone (a Gemma Stone Mystery)
Time Thieves

Published Non-Fiction Books:

Career Essentials
Career Essentials: The Résumé
Career Essentials: The Cover Letter
Career Essentials: The Interview
Career Essentials: 3 in 1

CPSIA information can be obtained
at www.ICGtesting.com
Printed in the USA
LVHW021731070620
657619LV00010B/753